diary of a 6th grade ninja 6

buchanan bandits!

BY **MARCUS EMERSON**
AND NOAH CHILD

ILLUSTRATED BY DAVID LEE

EMERSON PUBLISHING HOUSE

This one's for Parker...

STARRING
- CHASE (ME)
- ZOE
- GAVIN
- FAITH
- BRAYDEN
- NAOMI
w/special appearances by
Aliens & James Buchanan!

ALSO STARRING
- WYATT
- SEBASTIAN
- JAKE & THE WOLFPACK
- OLIVE
w/special appearances by
The Library Zombies!

There comes a point in everyone's life when they'll find themselves getting chased by a pack of ferocious werewolves. While I didn't think this was something that was going to happen to me until I was much older, say in *seventh* grade, I wasn't surprised to find it happening to me right at that moment.

My name is Chase Cooper, and I'm a sixth grade ninja… getting chased by werewolves.

THAT'S ME J
CHASE COOPER
(NINJA EXTRAORDINAIRE)

I sprinted through the dark forest as the tree branches slapped at my face as if they were against the idea of my escape. I'm not sure what I did to make the trees angry. Maybe it was because I carved my initials into one of their friends when I was younger – who knows?

Reaching behind my head, I pulled my ninja mask from the hood of my sweatshirt, slipping it over my cheeks until it completely covered my face.

With every step I took, I heard dry leaves crunch under my feet. I could also hear the same crunch from the pack of monsters closing in, and I knew there wasn't much time until they caught me.

"*Man, Chase is really out,*" I heard a werewolf say.

I wasn't sure what the monster meant by that, but I didn't want to find out.

"*Draw something on his face,*" another werewolf giggled. I could tell it was a girl by the sound of her voice.

The other monsters chuckled with her.

Panic washed over me at the thought of ink all over my forehead so I tried running faster, but it felt like my feet had started sinking in mud. I was still moving, but it was as if someone had hit the slow-motion button on my body. Since escape wasn't an option anymore, I spun in place, ready to face the incoming werewolves that were after me.

As their growls grew louder in my head, I clenched my fists. There was no way this ninja was going to go out like this.

At that second, the werewolves burst through the trees like violent water crashing against the shoreline. I braced myself for impact, setting my feet firmly in the ground, expecting a collision of epic proportions.

But instead of the impact happening in front of me, I felt an explosion of hot air come from *behind* me. The blast was so strong that the surrounding trees face-planted into the ground, flattening the werewolves into the earth the way that little plumber guy jumps on mushrooms in that one video game. I watched as the furry monsters blinked rapidly until bursting into a thousand tiny drops of light, fading out of existence.

It was s*uper* cool.

"*Chase Cooper!*" boomed a voice from the sky.

I turned slowly to face my enemy, afraid because I had a pretty good idea of what it was I was going to see. Crossing my fingers, I whispered to myself. "*Please* don't be a giant robot monster of President James Buchanan. *Please* don't be a giant robot monster of President James Buchanan! *Please!*"

But of course, standing before me, at nearly fifty feet tall, was *the giant robotic monster of President James Buchanan...* and he looked *angry*.

The robot raised one foot slowly and slammed it into the forest as he took a step forward. The ground shook again as he laughed heartily, arching his back like an evil villain.

As the robot's head sailed forward, I got a good look into his eyes, and saw exactly the kind of evil necessary to create a massive robot of destruction like the one in front of me. It was Wyatt, leader of the red ninja clan.

He was pulling on levers and pushing buttons inside one of the eyes of the robot, like he was handling some kind of oversized video game control.

WYATT

It was at that moment when a bunch of red ninjas teleported into existence around the robot's feet. Dozens of them materialized out of nowhere, and started rushing toward me with swords drawn.

I smirked, remembering my ninja training. I stepped forward and clapped my hands together as powerfully as I could, releasing a sonic boom of super sub-zero temperatures that turned every red ninja into frozen popsicles.

Don't ask me how it was done – it's a top-secret ninja move that involves crazy science… or something.

Suddenly, a voice cut through the air, squealing in fear. *"Somebody, help me!"*

My eyes narrowed, quickly scanning the monster until I saw the source of the plea. It was my friend, Faith! She was being held captive in the left hand of the robot. His grip must've been strong because she was struggling to free herself from it "Faith! Hang on, I'm coming to rescue you!" I shouted.

With my ninja skills, I leapt through the air, straight for President Buchanan's robot face. The air behind me caught fire from how quickly I was flying through space. Sticking my fist out, I aimed my body to make contact with the robot's eye, the one where Wyatt was comfortably sitting, probably sipping on a soda with a mouth full of snacks.

"Wyaaaaaaaaaatt!" was my battle cry as I shot forward.

"*Chase!*" Faith shouted. "*Look out for his other hand!*"

But it was too late. I was too focused on making it to Wyatt that I totally ignored the rest of the robot's body. President Buchanan's mighty robotic hand was the last thing I saw before it swatted me like a bug.

Instantly, my head sprang up. My arms shot forward as I struggled to catch myself before falling into the dark forest below me, which… wasn't there anymore. Instead of trees, I saw cold linoleum flooring. And instead of falling to my death, I was sitting on a bench. Staring forward, I blinked slowly, soaking in all the information I could. A pink block eraser was staring back at me.

…and so were all my friends.

Seated in the back of the cafeteria of Buchanan School, I watched as students devoured their food at tables across the room. It was lunchtime on Monday afternoon. I was always extra tired on Mondays and have been known to drift off during class from time to time. I patted at the pocket on my jeans, making sure my cell phone didn't fall out when I jumped awake. I was happy to see that it was still there.

"Good morning, sunshine!" Zoe, my cousin, said as she

grabbed the block eraser from the table. Zoe's one of the kindest, coolest kids on this planet. Even if she weren't my cousin, I think I'd still be friends with her, and that's saying a lot.

I rubbed the sore spot on my head, still too confused to talk. A small puddle of drool was left on the table where my face had been, and I could feel that my cheek was wet. Embarrassed, I dug my chin into my shoulder, trying to wipe the drool away, but only made it worse by smearing it all over my shirt.

"*Sick*, dude," Gavin laughed. Gavin used to be the captain of the hall monitors. He's a serious dude, and was also crucial in busting the kids responsible for wreaking havoc at the talent show awhile back. He's also going out with Zoe, which is… yuck.

Everyone else laughed with Gavin too. I knew my friends weren't actually making fun of me, but that didn't mean it *wasn't* embarrassing.

"What the *heck* were you dreaming about?" Zoe asked, smiling like she knew a secret.

I tripped over some words until I finally managed to form a sentence. "I, uh, it was nothing… really, it wasn't. Just something about werewolves and robot presidents controlled by a wavy haired kid."

Zoe tilted her head slightly, still grinning like a goon. "Was *Faith* in the dream?"

Faith sat across the table, covering her mouth, shocked at Zoe's question. Faith is *super* awesome. She's the only girl I knew who actually *wants* to play zombie FPS games. In fact, one time she brought over a pizza for lunch and we spent the afternoon playing ranked matches online. She upped my XP by at least 20!

"Great," I murmured. "Was I talking in my sleep again?"

"*Mumbling* is more like it. You *might've* said something about rescuing Faith at one point," Brayden said. Brayden was one of the first kids I became friends with a Buchanan. He's a wealth of knowledge when it comes to monsters, and is obsessed with werewolves, which is probably why they were in my dream.

Everyone laughed for a third time at Brayden's comment, even Faith, which actually helped me feel less embarrassed. If she were acting weird, then it would've been awkward, but since she was in on the joke, it was cool. I couldn't help but laugh a little myself.

"I always have weird dreams when I eat gummy bears before falling asleep," I said, and then added, "And I had, like, *a lot*. There's an *irresponsible* amount of gummy bears digesting in my belly right now."

"Bad dreams are the worst," Zoe commented.

"*Bad* dream? More like one of the most *awesome* dreams I've ever had!" I said, rubbing the sore spot on my noggin again. "Did one of you guys flick my head or something?"

Zoe held out the pink block eraser so I could see it. "I think Jake threw it."

Jake was seated at the table right behind ours. He spun around on his seat when he heard his name. "Enjoy your nap, little baby?"

Jake was easily one of the coolest kids at Buchanan, but that didn't make him "cool" by any means. He was one of the tough guys, always trying to pick on someone to make himself look awesome. As the star quarterback, all of the football team respected him, following him around like a pack of wolves, which is also why everyone called them the Wolf Pack.

To put it bluntly, Jake was a jerk.

Jake had targeted me ever since I switched the school's mascot from a wildcat to a moose. Okay, long story short – a few months ago I was given the opportunity to choose a new mascot for Buchanan. After a lot of thought, I chose the moose because those things are massive and majestic animals! Of course *now* I see how *uncool* a moose can be, but at the time I seriously thought I was doing something great!

A lot of the school was upset with my decision, but Jake took it personally since he was a rock star on the football team.

I wiped my mouth again, hoping there wasn't any more drool on my face.

"Go ahead and *keep* that eraser," Jake laughed. "I got a million of 'em!"

As always, I *wanted* to say something mean to him, but just couldn't bring myself to do it. "Thanks, man. That's very generous of you!"

"Nice burn," Faith muttered.

Before I could say anything else, the bell above the stage went off, signaling the end of lunch. If this were a normal week, then everyone would dump their trays and filter out of the cafeteria to go to their next class, but this week was going to be different.

This week was career week.

For the sixth graders at Buchanan School, the last half of each day was going to be spent in the cafeteria, learning about all

9

kinds of different careers. It was a way for us to gain some real world experience *way* before venturing out into the real world ourselves.

I'm normally against ideas like this just because I feel like it's a little forced, but in this case, I was really excited for it. Each student would get paired with a professional from whichever career they chose, and would learn about it throughout the rest of the week. A career *fair* was scheduled for the end of the week on Friday, which was basically a huge party for the last half of the day. I'm pretty sure it's the staff's way of rewarding themselves for a stressful week of students crammed into a cafeteria.

The school president, Sebastian, was the student in charge of the entire event. I know what you're thinking – if Sebastian is in charge of it, then it *must* be shady.

For those of you new to the story, allow me to quickly explain what I've had to deal with since my first day at Buchanan, but first we have to start with a kid named Wyatt who, if you remember, was piloting the robot James Buchanan.

During the first week of school, Wyatt recruited me into his ninja clan. Some bad stuff went down and I ended up taking control of his ninja clan. Ever since then, this kid has basically been a *splinter* in my *eyeball* and has recently started referring to me as his "sworn enemy."

Wyatt then started a second ninja clan that secretly trains in the abandoned greenhouse at the center of Buchanan School. The *red* ninja clan. They can tell each other apart when they're not in their ninja robes by the red bracelets they all wear.

Somehow, President Sebastian and Wyatt have become BFFs or something because Sebastian gave him the position of hall monitor captain, which is really why Gavin *lost* that position a couple months back.

It was possible that up until that point, Sebastian was just making poor decisions about who his friends were, but I soon found out that there was more going on than anyone realized. It was only last week that Gavin and I saw Sebastian hanging out with Wyatt *in* the greenhouse while the red ninjas trained.

Oh yeah, and get this – Wyatt's now the Vice President of Buchanan. Last week, a penguin named Hotcakes was lost in the school. *I'm* the one who found him, but *Wyatt's* the one who got credit for it, and what happened because of that? Sebastian gave him the position of VP right there on the spot. Everyone was so happy that Hotcakes was safe that they rejoiced at Wyatt's promotion.

Seriously? Those last four paragraphs would be the strangest thing I've ever written if they weren't the truth. Crazy school, huh?

President Sebastian is clearly in cahoots with Wyatt, but I had no idea how *or* why.

Anyway, the career week was entirely Sebastian's idea, and Principal Davis loved it so much that he ran with it. The truth was that everyone thought it was a great idea. Every student in the school was stoked to be a part of it, me included, which is how I found myself standing over one of the cafeteria tables that had a nametag with the words, "Chase Cooper," typed onto the front of it.

Glancing up, I saw that my table was next to the school supply shop, which was called "The Pit." The school thought it was a clever name because the reference was from those races where cars go around a track a million times. There's a spot on the track called the "*pit*" where cars could stop to refuel, get new tires, or get repaired quickly. Since the school supply shop was a place for students to buy snacks and school supplies, they named it "The Pit."

But the *students* of Buchanan called it "The Pit" because it was in the part of the cafeteria that stunk like an armpit. The shop was located in the far corner of the lunchroom, near the double door exit that led to the school dumpsters. The smell was horrendous, especially on hotter days. There had been times when it stunk so bad that it gave me a headache.

I pinched the clip on the back of my nametag and attached it to my shirt. Under the nametag was a manila folder with some sheets of paper tucked inside. Taking a seat, I flipped open the folder and took a peek.

There were some pamphlets that explained the job search process and some other ones about how pens are made. Is that a common job? Pen assembly?

"Can I have everyone's attention, please?" came Principal Davis's voice from the front of the cafeteria. He clapped his hands together. "Please everyone, eyes up here."

The room full of students slowly became silent. I saw Zoe and Faith a few tables down, sitting next to each other. Gavin and Brayden were also seated at another a table together. My jaw dropped as I let my shoulders slump. How come *they* got to sit together?

Principal Davis continued speaking. "If you'd all go ahead and find your places in the cafeteria, that'd be wonderful. You'll find your nametags along with a folder of other important items you'll need for the week. You'll need to clip your nametags to your shirts so that your mentors will know your name."

Nice! We were even going to get *mentors* – professionals from our chosen career field that were going to come and hang out with us during the week. I wondered if Principal Davis would have a hard time finding a real ninja for my mentor if that's what career I chose. Who am I kidding? *Of course* he'd have a hard time finding one because *you* don't find a ninja… a ninja finds *you*.

"Open your packets and take a look at the last sheet," Principal Davis said from the front of the room.

When I found the page he was talking about, I held it closer to my face. It was a thin slip of orange and white cardstock with numbers down the front of it. Next to each number was a set of four blank circles marked with the first four letters of the alphabet. It looked like a *test*.

"There's a sheet of questions for each student to fill out," Principal Davis said. "Once you're done with the questionnaire, you can leave them on the table for one of the staff to pick up. The results of your questionnaire will pair you with a career that's right for you so answer as honestly as you can."

"*What?*" I whispered hoarsely. "We don't get to *choose* our careers?"

A voice from the other side of the table replied. "You thought you could just write down '*ninja*,' and one would show up to this school?"

Before turning around, I already knew that it was Wyatt, and judging from the smell of spearmint, I was pretty sure his girlfriend, Olivia Jones, was right next to him. They're the weirdest couple I'd ever seen. Most of the time, they just stand at the side of the hallway between classes, holding hands and laughing maniacally. Imagine that for a second. Messed up, right?

"*Aloha*," Wyatt grinned when I made eye contact. I'm not sure why he used the Hawaiian word for "hello," but he did. I'm pretty sure the kid wasn't from Hawaii.

When he was the captain of the hall monitors, the school gave him an orange sash to wear so students would know who he was. Now that he was the vice president, he was wearing a sash with the words "VICE PRESIDENT" on it. But I'm pretty sure the school doesn't have a sash like that, which meant that Wyatt probably made it himself.

I nodded my head once just to acknowledge his presence. Seated next to him was Olive. I was right. She was chomping away on some chewing gum almost like she was *trying* to be annoying. She had so much gum in her mouth that she could barely chew with her lips shut! If she wasn't chewing so loudly, I probably would've been impressed!

I looked around, hoping a teacher was nearby because chewing gum at Buchanan was strictly forbidden. If it gets in the carpet, it's nearly *impossible* to get out. Not to my surprise, there wasn't a teacher in sight.

"Looks like we'll be sitting at the same table this week," Wyatt said, smirking.

I started to talk, but he spoke louder so he could drown my voice out.

"Hey, listen," Wyatt said, closing his eyes. "As the VP of Buchanan School, I think it's safe to say I'm not going to try anything crazy, okay? You can cool it, turbo."

The only way I was able to hold my tongue was by biting my lip. If I were going to have to spend a week next to him, it would probably be best if I didn't say anything I'd regret. I nodded again at him, "Deal."

Nobody else at our table even noticed that we had spoken to each other. They were all busy scratching their pencils on the test sheet, filling in circles with their number two pencils. Wyatt and Olive had started doing the same. I breathed a sigh of relief. Maybe this week wouldn't be so bad after all.

I scanned over the questions on the paper, and had to laugh at a few of them.

"Would you rather a) TRAIN an army of baby kangaroos or b) FIGHT an army of baby kangaroos?"

"Would you say you were a) a morning person, b) a night owl, or c) a machine sent back in time to fight the resistance?"

"If you could fist fight a zombie, would you? A) Yes. B) No."

I know, right? The questionnaire had a *hundred* of these kinds of bizarre questions!

After about twenty minutes of listening to Olive's gum chewing, I finally finished my career test. I flipped it over, spun on the bench, and faced the rest of the room, watching as other students finished their questionnaires as well.

A few students began walking aimlessly around the cafeteria. It wasn't like there wasn't anything to do. The staff had made sure to put up a bunch of workstations so kids could participate in different activities. Those stations kept most of the other kids busy.

I glanced across the room to see what Brayden and Gavin were doing, but they weren't at their table anymore. When I finally found them, they were huddled up with some other kids near the center of the cafeteria. Gavin had his brow furrowed as if he was concerned, but I'm pretty sure he always looked like that. It wasn't until I saw Brayden with the same expression that I knew something was wrong.

I stood from my table and joined the crowd of students. I was on the outside of the circle so I couldn't tell what was going on yet.

"What's up?" I asked Brayden.

Brayden shrugged his shoulders. "Somebody stole something, I think."

Gavin leaned over and stood on his tippy toes. "Not some*body*, but *a lot* of bodies. A *few* kids had some things stolen from them."

"Okay," I said, "so why isn't anyone speaking up about it? Why the weird huddle of whispers and secrets?"

"Because it was *gum* that was stolen," Faith said, as she stepped out of the circle and joined our conversation.

Zoe was right behind her. "Someone stole *gum* from *ten* different kids."

"Ah," Brayden sighed. "So it's not like they'd get help to begin with. If they admitted they had gum, they'd be asked *why* they even had it in the first place."

"Exactly," Faith said, rubbing her arms like she was cold.

"*Ten* kids?" I whispered. "Someone managed to get away with stealing gum from *ten* different people?"

Faith nodded. "Some of these kids had it taken right from their pockets too!"

"That's crazy!" I said. "That's…" I trailed off. I wanted to say it sounded like the work of a ninja, but I kept my mouth shut.

"What's crazy is that some of these kids said they still had their gum *before* answering the questions on that career test," Faith added. "That was only, like, twenty minutes ago."

Zoe darted her eyes at Wyatt as he approached. "It was *you*, wasn't it?"

"*What* was me?" Wyatt asked, annoyed.

As much as I didn't want to, I knew I had to speak up because it was the honorable thing to do. "No," I said, coming to Wyatt's defense. "He was with me the entire time, before *and* after the career test. He never left my sight." I pointed at Olive, who was still chomping away. "She was with him too, so it wasn't her either. Even though it *looks* like she's chewing enough gum for a football team, she was chewing on it before the career test."

Olive pushed the wad of gum into her cheek and stuck her tongue out at Zoe.

"*Nice*," Zoe said, disgusted and crinkling her nose.

Wyatt looked over his shoulder. I wasn't sure what it was about him, but it looked like he was hiding something. Knowing Wyatt, it was probably true.

Without saying another word, the leader of the red ninja clan turned and walked away with Olive by his side.

Gavin folded his arms, scowling. With his Texan accent, he spoke. "If it were just a single kid with th'problem, I'd be more inclined to ignore it, but since this involves nearly *ten* kids, then there's a strange pattern goin' on, ain't there?"

I smiled. "Yeah, we should investigate."

Zoe immediately chimed in. "No, that's dumb! How about just living a normal sixth grader life for once? No mysteries, no clues, no action, no adventure?"

"Right," I grumbled. "Because that's a *bajillion* times more fun."

"Bajillion's not a word," Zoe snipped.

I grumbled, lowering my head. "Is too."

"Is *not*," Zoe replied.

I paused, sitting in awkward silence for at least five seconds as our friends stood around. Finally, I whispered lower than anyone could hear. "*Is so.*"

Gavin raised his hands as if he were giving up. "Looks like I'm out," he said. "It's alright though. It's just a bit of stolen gum."

Just a bit of stolen gum? Didn't Gavin understand that the item that was stolen *wasn't* the point? The *point* was that something was *stolen*! Someone is going around stealing gum from people's book bags, which *shouldn't* be taken lightly, should it?

As Zoe and Gavin walked away, I felt my front pocket vibrate. I jumped, afraid that a bug was crawling up my leg before I realized it was my cell phone going off.

Since the last half of the day was devoted to the career week, I figured it wouldn't hurt to carry my phone with me. Good thing too, because I had just received a message.

I looked at the screen to see who the message was from, but it was sent by a number I didn't recognize.

Punching my four-digit password onto the front of my cell phone, I unlocked the screen and read the message.

> *"Meet me backstage ASAP. Come alone.*
> *- Wyatt"*

A girl snickered right next to me. It was Naomi, one of the most devoted members of my ninja clan. "*That* sounds like a good idea, right?"

I clicked the button on top of my phone, locking it again. Gavin was already on the other side of the room. Brayden was talking with Faith at another table. Naomi was the only one who knew I got a text from Wyatt. Slipping my phone back into my front pocket, I said something that surprised even *me*. "I think I'm gonna see what he wants."

Naomi's jaw dropped like it was DJ dropping the bass. "*Are you kidding me?*" she cried out.

Everyone nearby looked to see what she had screamed about.

Scratching the back of my head, I faked laughter as I led Naomi aside. When we were clear from the nosy students, I turned back to her and spoke. "I understand that my history with Wyatt hasn't been the best."

Naomi folded her arms. "You win the *understatement* of the *year* award! Congratulations! What do you plan on spending your prize money on?"

I laughed at her sarcasm.

Naomi's face switched from anger to concern. "You're not seriously going to meet with that psycho, are you?"

I paused to take a breath. "All I'm going to do is just go and *see* what he wants, is that so bad?"

Naomi's eyes grew fierce. "Then I'm going with you."

"That's not necessary," I said. "I'll be fine, really."

To my surprise, Naomi grabbed my forearm and started dragging me along with her. "Going alone isn't an option. I saw what he did to you during that first week of school, and I know what he's capable of. You're gonna need a friend if he snaps again."

"He's *not* gonna snap again," I said, but an uncomfortable feeling washed over me. What if he *did* snap again? "Alright, *maybe* it's a good idea for you to come with."

Naomi turned her head and smiled. "It was never an option."

Monday. 2:00 PM. Backstage in the cafeteria.

I took the lead, with Naomi following closely behind me. We decided it best to slip our ninja masks on when we were out of the sight from the rest of the students in the cafeteria. Since there was so much activity going on, none of the teachers saw us sneak through the heavy velvet curtains of the stage.

"After you," Naomi said, her voice muffled through the ninja mask. She held her hand out, gesturing across the dark stage for me to go first.

I crouched, taking the lead. "As your ninja leader, I'd think *you'd* want to go first to make sure everything was clear."

Naomi laughed. "Yeah, right. You're not *that* great of a leader."

"Kay," I said. "Just give me a minute. Sometimes when I'm nervous, I allow myself to feel like that for a full minute while I count the seconds."

Naomi's eye narrowed. "Whatever you say."

I shut my eyes and inhaled deeply. Feeling the muscles in my body relax, I began the countdown. "One hundred, ninety-nine, ninety-eight, ninety-seven—"

"I thought you said you only counted a *minute!*" Naomi hissed.

"I do!" I replied, annoyed by her interruption.

"But you started at a *hundred* seconds!"

"Yeah, a *minute.*"

Naomi continued to stare at me until it finally clicked in my

19

head.

"Oh right," I said, feeling rather silly. "Sixty seconds. Not a hundred."

My friend covered her mouth, holding in her laughter.

"Whatever," I said. "I'm more embarrassed than nervous now. Let's just go."

As we approached the back of the stage, I saw a soft red light coming from around the far corner of the stage, almost as if the light were guiding us, telling us where to go.

When we made it to the center, I glanced up, studying the curtain that loomed over us.

Naomi spoke softly, reading my thoughts. "You're thinking about the white ninja, aren't you?" she asked.

"Mm hmm," I hummed.

The white ninja had twice saved me from the red ninjas. The first time, he pulled me up and away from harm when I was getting chased. The second time, he dumped the curtain on a pack of red ninjas during the school's talent show just before they were about to beat the living daylights out of me.

"Do you know who it is?" Naomi asked.

"No," I replied. "I still have no idea, but I think he's on our side."

"What makes you think that?"

"Because he saved me... *twice*."

"That's doesn't mean anything," Naomi grunted. "Maybe he's playing you, making you *think* he's on your side."

"But why would he do that?"

"Who knows?" she answered. "I just think maybe you should just keep your guard up. This school seems to have it out for you."

"*Seriously, right?*" I said, turned back to her. "Like President Buchanan is haunting the halls of the school and is trying to ruin my life?"

I couldn't see Naomi's face, but I could see her eyes through the mask. She was looking at me like I was a crazy person. "*Riiiiiight,*" she sang. "I'm actually *not* surprised at the fact that you believe that."

I laughed again making it to the back of the stage, where the soft red light turned the corner. Carefully, I stepped down the short staircase and into the small hallway stacked with boxes from the drama club.

As soon as my foot touched the concrete, the red light clicked brighter. About ten feet away from Naomi and me was an old leather chair, facing away from us. Above the chair was a red light bulb swing slowly through the air, making the shadows on the floor expand and shrink. There was a weird burning smell in the air and suddenly I felt like I was a character that stupidly walked into a trap in one of those 80s horror movies.

"This is it," I whispered, feeling my stomach drop. "This is how I die…"

The chair spun in place, scaring the spew out of me. I jumped backward, accidentally bumping into Naomi.

"Our fearless leader," she joked.

The red light bulb flickered a couple times before switching colors to a bright white. I squinted my eyes, trying to see who was in the chair.

"Dude," Wyatt said, leaning back in the leather chair. He wasn't wearing his ninja outfit. "Relax, it's just *me*. I mean, you *knew* it was me that wanted to meet you back here, right? I signed the text message with my name."

"But you didn't have to make it feel like I was walking into a freaky nightmare!" I said through my mask.

Wyatt chuckled. "Right, sorry about that," he said, pointing at the light. "That old bulb really needs to be replaced." The leader of the red ninjas spun in his chair again, raising a hand to someone hiding in the darkness. "Is it ready yet?"

I thought maybe it was Olive, but it wasn't.

"Almost, sir," a boy's voice said from the shadows.

I pulled my mask off and tucked it away in the hood of my sweatshirt. "What is this? What's that smell?"

As if answering my question, a boy wearing a suit stepped from the shadows, handing Wyatt a porcelain plate. A Belgian waffle sat on top of the dish, steaming hot and fresh.

Let me say that again in case you missed it… it was *a Belgian waffle.*

"Would you like one?" Wyatt asked, as if getting handed a freshly cooked waffle backstage and in the middle of the school day was a totally normal thing to happen. I guess being the vice president had its perks.

The boy in the suit sprayed a can of whipped cream over the top of Wyatt's food. I seriously felt like I was losing my mind. I shook my head, remembering my reason for being there. "*Why did you text me? What do you want?*"

Wyatt took a bite from the breakfast food. With a cheek full of waffle, he pointed his fork at Naomi and said, "I *told* you to come alone."

"You're *lucky* I'm here at all," I said.

Wyatt stopped chewing and looked at me like he was a confused dog. "I'm sorry, what did you say? I couldn't hear you over the sound of my own awesomeness."

"You mean the sound of you chewing with your mouth fully open?" Naomi said. "I'm *flabbergasted* as to how *no* food is falling on your lap."

"If you want to talk to me," I said boldly, "then Naomi gets to stay."

Swallowing his bite, Wyatt nodded. "Fine," he said. "Naomi is cool. She's a good ninja. I remember her from when I was the leader of your clan."

"You mean when you were the leader for, like, less than a week?" Naomi scorned. It was obvious that she wasn't afraid of Wyatt, and her little remarks helped make me feel more at ease with having a conversation with him.

"You fool!" Wyatt snapped like some kind of villain. "Don't you realize your *insults* only make me *stronger?*"

I said nothing, but Naomi giggled at Wyatt's little outburst.

Wyatt held his plate of food out as he inhaled slowly, calming himself down. The boy in the suit took it from him, replacing it with a tiny green item.

"I want to call a truce," Wyatt said as he held out the green speck for me to see. It was a four-leafed clover. "I assume you remember the first task I ever assigned to you?"

I stared at the clover. "You said if I wanted to join your ninja clan, I had to return to the hideout with one of those."

Wyatt nodded. "Totes," he said, shortening the word *"totally."* "And that's why I'm presenting it to you right now – to show you I'm serious about the truce."

I glanced at Naomi. She was staring at the clover too, unsure of what to make of it.

"Why?" I asked sternly. "Why a *truce?* Why *now?* Also – do you think I'm *dumb?*"

"No," Wyatt answered straight-faced. "I *don't* think you're dumb. In fact, I *know* you're more clever than I am, which is why you're here."

"Get to the *point*," Naomi demanded.

Wyatt grunted, staring at her, and then turned his attention back to me. "The gum theft has sparked my interest, and I'm asking for a truce so that the two of us can work together to find the… *bandit.* It's obvious that there's something fishy going on with that, and I'd like to get to the bottom of it. You know that Olive and I are an item, and you also know how much she loves her gum. I'd like to figure this out… to keep *her* from becoming a victim of the Buchanan bandit. Clever, right? I *just* coined that term. Like, *just* now."

23

"You want our ninja clans to team up?" I asked, completely dumbfounded.

Wyatt shook his head. "*No*, not our ninja clans. Just *us*. You and me. Two people."

I didn't need to waste another second thinking about it. "No way," I said coldly. "There's no way I can trust you. You've burned me too many times for that."

Clenching his jaw, Wyatt spoke through his teeth. "I believe this bandit situation is bigger than any of us know. Don't come running back to me when this whole thing blows up in your face."

"Right. This whole thing is gonna blow up in my face," I replied with as much sarcasm as I could muster. I turned my back on him and headed back to the cafeteria. Naomi turned and followed my lead, leaving Wyatt in the beat up leather chair with his waffle cook.

"You'll be sorry," Wyatt sneered as we walked away.

It took all my strength to look like I had it together, but the truth was that I *didn't* have it together. With my history at Buchanan, the entire situation *could* blow up in my face, and that scared me to my core.

Monday. 2:20 PM. The cafeteria.

When we were away from the stage, Naomi playfully punched my arm and said I had made the right decision. Deep down, I knew that I did, but I still couldn't help but feel like I had made a mistake by not accepting Wyatt's help.

I took a seat on the edge of the stage, staring at nothing, going over every word of Wyatt's conversation in my head. Was it possible that Wyatt was really offering a truce? And if he was, what then? Was I supposed to forget everything that's happened before any of this? Is that what adults mean when they say to *forgive and forget?*

The problem was that I still didn't fully trust him, but can you blame me? One afternoon and a Belgian waffle was supposed to make us BFFs?

"Something's wrong," Zoe stated.

I rubbed my eyes, bringing my head down from the clouds. "Huh?" I grunted. "What's the matter? What's wrong?"

"No," Zoe said, letting out a breath of air through her nose. She hopped onto the stage and took a spot next to me. Together, we watched the students in the cafeteria live their totally normal lives in a school they didn't realize *wasn't* so normal. "I mean, something's wrong with *you.*"

Being my cousin, Zoe could read me like a book. I debated whether or not to tell her about Wyatt, but ultimately decided it was best if she didn't know… at least for that moment. "Yeah, I mean, no," I said. "Nothing's wrong with me."

"Chaaaaaase," she sang. "C'mon, don't be such a baby. Just tell me what's going on."

I took a second to respond. "I was just wondering… isn't life supposed to get back to normal after some kind of crazy event?"

"You mean how Wyatt became the vice president?" she asked.

"Sorta," I said, bobbing my head back and forth. "I mean, once the day is saved, things should go right back to normal, shouldn't they? I've saved the day quite a few times at this school, and it doesn't ever seem to go back to the way things were *before* anything crazy happened. When I found the red ninja clan, they didn't disappear after that. When Wyatt became the hall monitor captain, he *stayed* the hall monitor captain! And now he's *still* the vice president! Shouldn't he just go back to being a bully with no power?"

"Um, yeah," Zoe said, raising an eyebrow. "That's because this is real life, and not a television show. The universe doesn't reset at the end of the day. You've watched too much TV. Things change – life *changes*, and you have to adapt."

I tried my best to think of an example. "You mean, like, the way a video game changes its difficulty setting if you're too good?"

Zoe stared at me for a moment. "No," she finally said. "Not like that."

I sighed, feeling like my body was sinking into itself.

Zoe kept talking. "I think I'd go crazy if things went back to normal at the end of every day."

"Why?" I asked, curious.

"It just sounds so… *boring*, doesn't it? If life didn't move forward, then nothing could ever grow."

"Ugh," I groaned. "A *flower* analogy?"

"No, *dork*," Zoe said. "I mean that *we* would never grow. *We'd* stay the same boring immature kids forever without ever having gone through a single challenge. We wouldn't be forced to overcome and strengthen ourselves through mistakes or failures."

The bell to the school rang over our conversation, which meant it was the end of the school day.

Zoe bounced up and turned back to face me. "You know

26

what I mean?"

I stood from the stage and nodded. "I think so," I said.

Zoe smiled as she spun around again. Once she located Gavin with some kind of girl radar in her head, she jogged off. I joined the swarm of students walking toward the exit of the cafeteria.

Maybe Zoe was right. Maybe life *shouldn't* reset at the end of every episode. I wouldn't be who I was if it weren't for the crazy year I've had so far, right? It was right there when I decided that maybe siding with Wyatt was a *good* idea, but if it wasn't then it was a mistake that I'd have to learn from.

Besides, it was actually possible that Wyatt had changed his ways, wasn't it?

Tuesday. 7:35 AM. Before homeroom.

When I got to school, I went straight for my locker like any normal sixth grader would do. Digging through the trash heap in my locker, I found the right textbooks for my morning classes and actually found a pen that wasn't dried out so I slipped that into my book bag too.

The nametag I had been given the day before had a little metal clip on the end of it, which I attached to one of the laces on my shoe. I didn't feel like clipping it to my shirt, and I felt like my shoe was just the better place for it.

My plan was to find Wyatt and try to continue the conversation we had backstage in the cafeteria. I felt a little uneasy about it, but I kept reminding myself that people *could* change.

As I zipped up my bag, I overheard some kids talking as they walked behind me.

"Did you hear that Jesse's gum got stolen too?"

"No way! So did Matt and Rachel's! Right from their backpacks, which is weird because Rachel said she keeps her lunch money in the same pocket as her gum, but the money wasn't even touched!"

"I know, right? A friend of mine keeps his gum in a small pouch along with the rest of his candy, but only *the gum was taken!"*

The conversations were like that in every hallway I walked down. There was something crummy going on, that was for sure. If it were just a couple kids with the problem, it'd be one thing, but now that it sounds like almost everyone in the school is a victim, it's become a spree.

The strangest part about it was that the Buchanan bandit was *only* taking gum, which is pretty smart if you ask me. The bandit probably knows kids won't say anything because it's something *they* shouldn't have either.

But even as I walked to homeroom, I noticed that a bunch of kids were actually chewing on gum right at that moment. At first I thought those students were the bandits until I realized the ones who were chomping were completely random kids, spread out down the hallway. None of them were part of the same groups, which could only mean they weren't victims... *yet.*

Just then, I felt someone nudge against my back. I sighed, feeling my stomach turn because I thought it was going to be someone I didn't want to see. Thankfully, I was wrong.

"Sorry, man," said another sixth grade boy. I recognized him from the school, but I had never spoken to him before. He sulked back, keeping his hands cupped and close to his chest.

"No problem-o," I said, tightening a smile. In his hands was a pink block eraser, actually *two* block erasers – they were the same kind that nailed my noggin the day before, waking me from my slumber. They were so bright that they were impossible to miss. "Cool erasers."

The boy shot me a dirty look. "Keep your grubby paws off them! They're mine!" he growled.

I stood, stupefied. "They're just erasers."

"I said they're mine!" the boy shouted, licking the sides of both erasers. When he was done, he stared at me with raised eyebrows like he had just won an argument we never had.

"Alright, man," I said, breaking eye contact. "Whatever."

"That's right," he said as I walked away. "They're *mine.*"

I didn't look back at him, but I could feel his eyes burning holes in the back of my head. "Weirdo," I whispered.

Tuesday. 7:45 AM. Homeroom.

The bell rang just as I set foot in the door to my homeroom class. I even dove into my seat before it *stopped* ringing. Yeeeeeah… ninja skills.

Zoe was seated in front of me, and Brayden was at his usual place in the seat to my left. His head was buried in his arms on the desk, the common sign to leave someone alone because they were trying to catch a nap. It might be the common sign for crying too. I don't know.

Mrs. Robinson, the homeroom teacher, was playing with a brown paper bag on her desk while the rest of the students waited patiently. Finally, she patted a stack of papers together, leaned back, and started giving the morning announcements.

"Good morning, students," Mrs. Robinson said loudly. "Today is day two of our career week, and assuming everything goes as it should, your test results should be in and you ought to get paired with a mentor from your chosen field."

"Not chosen by *us*," I whispered sarcastically, leaning my head forward so Zoe could hear me.

My cousin shrugged her shoulders, but continued facing the front of the room.

Mrs. Robinson continued. "So just like yesterday, classes will be normal up until after lunch, when all the sixth graders will meet in the cafeteria." She paused, studying her sheet of notes, trying to make sense of something on the page. "I guess all the mentors will already be at your table? I'm sorry, the memo isn't too clear on that part."

Nobody in the class seemed to mind.

Standing from her desk, Mrs. Robinson walked to the front of the room with the brown paper sack in her hand. The way she was gripping the bag, it was obvious it was filled with something heavy.

"And as an added bonus," Mrs. Robinson said, "Buchanan School is giving a block eraser to every sixth grader today."

The room fell silent for a moment – the kind of silent that would creep you out in a movie theater just before the monster jumps onto the screen. Everyone looked at each other, confused. But all of a sudden, the room exploded with cheers and shouts of joy.

Brayden's body jerked. He grabbed the sides of his desk and looked panicked. I laughed because I was sure that was exactly how I looked during lunch the other day.

The homeroom teacher counted out each row of students and handed the kid in the first seat a stack of erasers. "Take one and pass the rest back," she said.

"What just happened?" Brayden asked, staring into space.

"A werewolf was just spotted north of here," Zoe joked with a straight face. "A team of special forces has been dispatched and are hoping to capture the beast alive."

Brayden blinked. I could see life returning to his face. "Nuh-uh," he said.

Zoe and I let out a short laugh.

"Seriously," Brayden said. "Nuh-uh, right?"

"What do *you* think?" Zoe asked, turning in her chair.

Brayden fell silent for a second.

"OMG," Zoe said, shaking her head and smiling. "*No*, they didn't find a werewolf, alright? I was joking."

Brayden pressed his lips together as he rubbed his forehead. "Don't even *joke* about that," he said. "So why'd everyone freak out just now?"

Zoe turned in her chair. "Everyone's getting a block eraser."

"No," Brayden said. "I mean, why did everyone *shout* like that?"

Zoe raised her eyebrows at him and repeated herself. "Because… *everyone's getting a block eraser.*"

31

"Oh," Brayden replied. "Cool… I guess."

"Yeah, what's the deal with those things?" I asked. "I saw someone before school with a couple of them. He kinda freaked when I mentioned them. And then he… *licked* 'em."

"Sick." Zoe smirked as she took two erasers from the student in front of her. She turned back and joked, "They're what's *hot* in the *streets*. Haven't you heard? You ain't cool unless you got one of these pink blocks."

"But they're just erasers," I said, taking the last one from Zoe's hand. "Who cares?"

Brayden smiled as he studied his eraser. "You collect comics, right?"

"Right," I replied.

"Well, think of these erasers like that," Brayden explained. "Remember a couple years ago when everyone was collecting those rubber band bracelets shaped like random things?"

I smiled, tilting my head slowly and acting like I was remembering a fond memory. "Yeaaaaaah. Those dinosaur ones were *bananas*."

Zoe laughed. "Dork."

"Still though," I said, staring at the pink block in my hand. "I just don't see the appeal in these things."

Before our conversation was over, the bell chimed outside the door. Everyone in the room pulled their book bags over their shoulders and poured out of the room.

Tuesday. 10:30 AM. Before gym class.

On my way to gym, I always made sure to take the hallway on the east side of school. The gymnasium was in that direction, but Faith also has a class over there. Talking to her was always a good way to kill some time before class.

When I found her, Gavin was standing next to her already in the middle of a conversation.

"S'up, noob?" Faith asked as she leaned against the lockers outside her classroom.

"The *sky*," I answered, regretting it immediately. My brain screamed at me, "*Why do you keep trying to make that funny? It's not funny! It's never been funny, and it never* will *be funny! As punishment, here's some forehead sweat!*" And yeah, the top of my forehead *did* start to sweat.

Faith laughed anyway.

"Nice," Gavin said.

Changing the subject, I spoke while pointing at Gavin. "Actually I was hoping to find you. I still think we should try and figure out who's been nabbing all the gum."

Gavin was quick to respond. "Nuh-uh, no sir. I told ya yesterday, I can't be a part of all that this time. Zoe made a pretty good point in saying we shouldn't get involved. Remember what happened last time? We found a secret ninja hideout fulla red ninjas training."

"For serious?" Faith asked, intrigued. "You did?"

I shut my eyes and sighed. "*Maybe.*"

33

"All this just seems like more trouble than it's worth," Gavin said. "You know what sounds good to me? Having a normal school day. The kind of day where ya get to school hoping to catch some rest and relaxation, zoning in and out of a daze until the clock hits 2:35. *That* sounds like an excellent day."

I was disappointed to hear Gavin say that. Out of all my friends, I thought for sure, *he'd* be the one who would want to seek justice. "But *something* is going on, right?" I asked. "Isn't it strange that a *ton* of kid's gum is getting stolen, and *only* gum?"

Gavin paused. "*Only* gum, huh?"

I squeezed my fist. Gavin *was* interested. I could tell by the twinkle in his eye.

Shaking his head, Gavin glanced at his wristwatch. "No, I can't. I'm sorry, but I just can't."

"Bummer," Faith said as she watched Gavin walk away.

"I know, right?" I replied.

Faith fell silent for a second, and then she spoke softly. "My gum was stolen this morning too."

My heart sunk. "No way. Why didn't you say anything?"

"I'm saying it now," Faith replied. "It was in my pocket and everything."

"They managed to get it from your *pocket?*"

Faith nodded. "During the break between homeroom and first period. I had it when I left homeroom, and when I got to first period, it was gone."

"Did anything happen to you during that break? Anyone bump into you?"

Faith turned her lips to one side of her face and took a breath. "Nope. Not a single strange thing happened. Nobody bumped into me. Nobody even talked to me."

This was serious. This *wasn't* just a bandit, but a *skilled* bandit... maybe even a *ninja* bandit. And not that it wasn't a big deal before, but now the bandit had stolen from a *friend* of mine, it affected me on a personal level, and I found myself getting even more annoyed by it.

"Maybe he's right though," Faith said, pointing in the direction that Gavin had walked away in. "Maybe this is a case *not* worth investigating. I'm not even mad. It was a pack of gum that cost me a quarter."

"It might be *just* a cheap pack of gum," I said, "but that's *not* the point. The point is that someone thinks it's okay to steal other people's stuff. *Something* has to be done. All it takes for bad guys to win is for the good guys to do *nothing*. I don't want to be the guy that just stood by and did *nothing*."

"You know what else is considered 'doing something?'" Faith asked.

I waited for her answer, but I already knew what she was going to say.

"Telling the principal," she finally said.

"But he *won't* do anything," I said defensively. "*None* of the staff will because nobody's supposed to have gum anyway."

Faith shrugged her shoulders, but didn't say anything else about it.

Again, the bell rang chimed, blaring loudly in my ear. Faith smiled and gave me a quick hug, telling me not to do anything stupid. I promised her I'd try my best.

I was already late to gym, but since it was right down the hall, it wasn't a big deal. That was the one class where everyone showed up late anyhow. Coach Cooper never really cared.

This *Buchanan bandit* situation was starting to look more like an epic disaster rather than a petty theft. It might seem like a silly thing to worry about because, like Faith said, "It's just a pack of gum," and while just a pack of gum might be a lame sounding crime, it gets a lot worse when it becomes a *boatload* of gum.

I wonder what a boatload of gum would even look like.

Tuesday. 10:45 AM. The locker room.

Since I was one of the last ones in gym, the locker room was pretty empty by the time I made it to the aisle my locker was in. Coach Cooper was sitting behind the computer in his office, playing that card game everyone plays. I can never remember what it's called, but when you beat it, the cards bounce all over the screen. *Thrilling*, right?

Turning the corner, I walked down the aisle to my locker. I was deep in thought, holding my book bag straps tight around my shoulders.

During the first week of school, Wyatt was in the same gym class as I was. After he returned to school, they put him in another class. How strange that I was actually *wishing* we were in the same class again. It would make finding him much easier.

I craned my neck to the side, cracking it as I let my book bag drop to the floor. The thump of canvas echoed off the green lockers in the empty room.

Coach Cooper had closed the game on his screen, and must not have noticed that I hadn't left the room yet. He always stayed until the last kid left, probably to make sure nobody got into anything they shouldn't have. Oh well. At least it was quiet.

Clutching the dial on my locker, I spun the combination. Gripping the metal latch, I was about to pull up until something caught my eye. I froze, feeling my legs get numb.

Someone had taped a note to the top of my locker.

It wasn't the first time someone left me a note, and it

36

probably wouldn't be the last time either.

I glanced over my shoulder making sure I actually *was* alone. When it was clear, I snatched the slip of paper into my hands and unfolded it.

"Keep your nose outta our business, or else."

I chuckled loudly, in case the person who left the note was still in the room. I didn't want to show any sign that I was afraid or intimidated. I even spoke out loud. "*Pssssh!* Or else *what*?"

The answer to my question came when I opened the metal door of my gym locker. I pulled up on the latch, flipping the container open. My jaw dropped as I stared at the wall of stolen gum packages that had been crammed so tightly into the small space that they didn't even fall out. They were like tiny bricks that stunk of spearmint.

"So *that's* what a boatload of gum looks like," I whispered.

Immediately I slammed the door shut. The sound of clanging metal screamed across the locker room. Luckily there wasn't anyone in there.

"What's your problem, lame wad?" a voice said from behind me.

At least I *thought* there wasn't anyone in there.

I set my hand on the cold metal surface of my locker. "Heh, nothing," I said in an embarrassingly high pitched voice. "Sorry 'bout that. Sometimes I don't know my own strength!"

The boy glared at me as he moved in slow motion. Finally, he rolled his eyes. "Whatever," he said before leaving the locker room.

I felt my heart pound inside my chest, and for some reason I couldn't catch my breath. There I was, alone in the boy's locker room, with a locker filled with stolen gum. I wish I could say it was a situation that was new to me, but I couldn't.

This entire situation escalated way too quickly. First it was a pack of stolen gum, then it was *many* packs of stolen gum, and now someone's zeroed in on *me* specifically.

Why do these things always happen to *me*?

I sat, defeated, on the bench in the center aisle, but felt something underneath me. When I slid over, I saw a red bracelet. The same red bracelet that Wyatt's red ninjas always wore.

I picked it up, thinking that maybe one of the red ninjas was behind the stolen gum, but then realized it was pretty unlikely. If a red ninja had planted the gum in my locker, then there was *no way* they'd be foolish enough to forget their red bracelet at the scene of the crime.

RED NINJA BRACELET

Another possibility was that whoever was trying to frame me was *also* trying to frame the red ninja clan. It was like they thought, "Oh I'll just leave this red bracelet here. That way Chase will believe the red ninjas did it!"

Too bad for them, I'm not as dumb as I am…

I mean, as dumb as I *think* I am…

No wait, as dumb as *they* think I am.

Nevermind.

That was now another reason for me to seek Wyatt's help, but I didn't want to wait until after lunch to find him. I needed to get ahold of that kid ASAP, and I'm pretty sure I knew where to find him.

Tuesday. 11:00 AM. Outside the red ninja hideout.

Coach Cooper let me out of class without even flinching. The craziest part was that I didn't even try to hide the truth. I said there was a situation that needed to be dealt with concerning some stolen goods, and that I wanted to find Wyatt to talk about it. The coach waved his hand and wished me luck.

Crazy, right?

It took me a few minutes to get backstage in the cafeteria. The first time I stumbled upon the red ninjas hideout was when I was chasing after the missing penguin a week ago. The bird had escape through a secret passage in the hall that led back to an abandoned greenhouse.

If you would've told me last week that I'd *willingly* walk into the red ninja's hideout, I would've laughed until tears streamed down my cheeks.

The only thought going through my head was, *"What am I doing? What am I doing? What am I doing?"*

Finally, I made it to the opening of the greenhouse. I could hear their thumps and hollers as they trained together. It sounded a lot like I was standing outside a dance club. Leaning against the wall, I reconsidered what it was I was doing. Listening to the sound of the training red ninjas didn't help me feel better.

On the floor next to the opening were red ninja robes, folded nicely and stacked on top each other. I had to hand it to them – the red ninjas were a very organized, tidy bunch of kids. My own clothing at home wasn't even folded!

I stretched my arms out behind my back, whispering to myself. "Am I really gonna do this? Am I really gonna put on a red ninja outfit?"

Staring at the folded robes on the floor, I sighed. "Yep, I sure am."

Tuesday. 11:02 AM. The red ninja hideout.

It only took about two minutes for me to slip into the red ninja robes. Wyatt had designed them to go right over their street clothes. It was pretty smart actually, and I was a little jealous that I hadn't thought of it first. I took the red bracelet out of my pocket and held it tightly in my hand.

I stepped in front of the opening to the greenhouse, and without a second thought, forced myself to enter.

The smell of dead plants lingered in the air, along with the scent of kids getting their sweat on by training. It was more musty than stinky.

As I passed by other ninjas, they glanced at me, nodding their head as a greeting. I punched my open palm and nodded back at them.

From where I was standing, I could see Wyatt sitting in his beat up leather chair at the front of the greenhouse. He wasn't wearing *any* of his ninja gear, which wasn't too surprising. As the VP, he probably didn't want to risk getting caught wearing it. With an intense stare, he studied his ninjas as they threw punches and kicks into the air.

Sifting through the crowd of red ninjas, I made my way to the front of the room, hoping nobody would recognize me. I'm not sure how they would since I was fully decked out in red ninja—

"Hey!" shouted one of the bigger red ninjas. He stepped in front of me, blocking my path to Wyatt.

"Not good," I whispered.

"What do you think you're doing?" the ninja growled with a more feminine voice that I had originally heard. It was a girl under the mask. She was holding her fist at me.

I wasn't sure how to respond, so I didn't say anything. By this time, everyone in the room was staring at me, *including* Wyatt from the front of the greenhouse.

"I said, *what* do you think you doing?" the tall girl repeated.

My whole world was crumbling around me as a billion different emotions shot through my body. If I ran, I *might* be able to make it out of the room before they started chasing after me.

It was a personal decision I made long ago to never throw a punch, but I wasn't sure any of the ninjas surrounding me made the same decision. I was as good as dead.

The big ninja pointed at the bracelet that was in my death grip. "You *wear* that thing with *pride*. It goes on your wrist, dummy!" the ninja joked, laughing heartily.

The other ninjas in the greenhouse laughed with her.

The room started spinning as I gasped for air. Apparently my brain put my lungs on pause – it does dumb things like that sometimes. I tried laughing too, covering up the fact that I was actually catching my breath, as I pulled the bracelet over my wrist. I only hoped they couldn't see how badly my hands were shaking.

"I'm just messin' witch'ya," the giant girl said before finally lumbering off.

I swallowed hard, looking back at Wyatt who was still in his leather chair. Casually, I walked the rest of the way to the front of the room and stood by his side.

ME
(DECKED OUT IN RED NINJA GEAR)

WYATT'S CHAIR

WYATT

Wyatt didn't move a muscle. His head was resting in one hand as he watched the red ninjas train in the room. He almost looked bored.

Struggling with what to say, I leaned closer to him, but he spoke before I did.

"Great day for training," the leader of the red ninja clan said. "Isn't that right, Chase?"

My jaw tightened, and I felt like I couldn't move again. At last, I asked, "How'd you know?"

Wyatt spun his chair around to face me. "You don't move

the way my red ninjas move. You've got a different way about you."

I wasn't sure whether to be proud of that fact or not.

Wyatt pointed at my shoes. "Plus you're wearing a slip of paper that has your name on it."

I looked down at the nametag I had clipped to my shoe that morning. "Stupid," I whispered, scolding myself.

"Don't sweat it," Wyatt said, chuckling. "But you'd better get talkin' before anyone else in here figures out who you are. I'd tell them to leave you alone, but in a group this big, they might not hear me over the sound of their own anger."

I took his advice, and began explaining myself right away. For the next few minutes, I told him about how the gum bandit was taking more than anyone realized, and how they're only focused on gum instead of other things that actually have *value*.

"And right now my friends have decided to sit this one out," I said, "but I didn't want to investigate alone… so that's why I'm here – too see if your offer still stands."

"My offer to help?" Wyatt asked.

I nodded, remaining in place at his side. The rest of the red ninjas in the room continued training without a clue about what was happening at the front of the greenhouse.

"Admit that you were wrong" Wyatt demanded.

I said nothing.

He smirked the same way I'd imagine an evil overlord would right before claiming victory over the world. "*Tell* me I was right."

Not wanting to waste any more time in the greenhouse, I clenched my teeth. "Fine. You *weren't* wrong."

Wyatt paused, studying me with his narrow eyes. "Good enough for me!"

"So that's that then?" I asked. "Just like that and we're working together?"

Wyatt spun again in his chair, grabbing a small box from the ground. "Not quite," he said. "You burned me yesterday when you refused my offer first. I even went through the trouble of finding a four-leafed clover to show how serious I was."

"Okaaaaay," I said, suspicious of his motives. "So?"

Wyatt's face grew angry, but he kept his voice down. "So *you* have to do something for me to show me that *you're* serious!"

"You want a four-leafed clover? I'll get you a four-leafed clover," I said, even though it was Zoe that found the clover back at the beginning of the year.

"No," Wyatt said, tapping his fingers on the cardboard box in his lap. "All you have to do is take this to the principal's office."

"Yeah?" I asked. "That's *all* I have to do, huh? Is that box filled with money or something?"

That was part of my first week at Buchanan too. Taking a bag full of money to the principal's office to frame my cousin Zoe for theft.

Wyatt peeled open the top of the box and grabbed a handful of what was inside. They were the block erasers that everyone was going nuts over, but this box contained more than just pink ones. "I promise you that this is only filled with these dumb little things."

"What's the deal with those anyway?" I asked, suddenly aware of a nasty spearmint scent in the air. I glanced at the red ninjas in the room and wondered which one of them was Olive.

"These little rubber block erasers are Sebastian's own

creation," Wyatt explained. "He created these to coincide with the career week stuff. It's all about sales and marketing and blah blah blah, y'know?"

"So *he's* the one handing these things out?"

"He's *selling* them," Wyatt said.

"How's he allowed to do that?" I asked.

Wyatt sighed. "For every eraser sold, he donates ten cents to the school. Since they're selling so well, the school is considering selling them through the school supply shop for a buck a pop."

"A dollar?" I said loudly. "He's making *ninety cents* off these things? But my homeroom teacher handed out a ton of these for *free* this morning!"

Wyatt laughed. "That's right. The school *bought* all those erasers from Sebastian so they could do that. I guess Principal Davis is all for the idea of Sebastian starting a business, especially because of all the career stuff this week. There's probably a great lesson to be learned here about money and economics, but… whatever, I don't care."

I took one of the erasers in my hand and looked at it. It was a bright blue color with a thin piece of cardstock wrapped around it. Sebastian's picture and logo were also on the paper. "I gotta hand it to the kid, he knows how to sell a product."

"Right?" Wyatt said as he shoved the box of rubber blocks into my hands. "So get this to the principal's office. There's nothing shady about my request. They know the box is coming, and I'm just too lazy to take it there myself," he said smiling, and holding his hand out for me to shake it.

Without hesitating, I grabbed my enemy's hand and shook it like a businessman.

Heading for the exit, I nodded at a few of the red ninjas as I left. They still didn't have a clue who I was.

Once I was clear of the greenhouse, I took off the red ninja robes, dumping them in one of the drama club boxes backstage. With the block erasers in my arms, I stepped into the cafeteria and headed straight for the front offices.

Tuesday. 11:25 AM. The front offices.

When I walked into the air-conditioned front office, a younger woman with blonde hair tied back in a ponytail greeted me. I'd never seen her before, but that wasn't weird since she probably didn't teach any classes at Buchanan.

"Can I help you?" she asked, standing at the counter and chewing the end of her pencil.

I set the box of erasers on the counter and flipped open the lid. "I'm supposed to drop these off here, I guess?"

The woman's smile was bright enough to light up a dark room. "*Fantastic!* We've been waiting all morning for these! Principal Davis will be thrilled."

"Cooooooooool," I said suavely. "So I'll just leave them with you, and that's all?"

"That's all," the woman replied sliding the box off the other side of the front counter. "Just tell me your name so I can let Principal Davis know who delivered them. I know he'll want to know how helpful you were."

With a smile beaming across my face, I said, "Chase Cooper."

"Thanks, Chase," the woman said.

I turned around just in time to hear the lunch bell sound off. Before the front lobby could completely swarm with students, I managed to make it across the hall so I could stand in front of the tinted windows of the cafeteria and wait for my friends.

"Over here!" Faith shouted in front of the lunchroom doors.

Brayden and Gavin stood behind her, waiting in the lunch line. Zoe wasn't around, which meant that she was probably in the library with the other zombies.

And yes, I *did* just said zombies.

The smart kids in the school, aka "smarties," were allowed to sit in the library during lunch so they could have an extra study period during the day. It was *meant* to be a reward so they could spend the time doing extra research for any papers or projects they might've been working on. It was the only time during the day when surfing the Internet on your cell phone was allowed. The hope was that the smarties would appreciate the responsibility and use their time wisely.

The reality of it though, was that pretty much all the smarties spent the entire time staring at their cell phones, texting friends and sharing dumb videos of cute animals doing silly things. Have you ever seen kids hypnotized by a five-inch cell phone screen? They look like zombies, which is where the name came from.

Zoe claims she actually uses that time for research, but I know better. She's just as zombified as the rest of them when she's in there.

A short while back, I had found myself in the midst of the library zombies, and trust me, it's a lot scarier than it sounds. After that fateful day, I vowed never to return to the land of the library zombies.

Meeting up with Faith, Gavin, and Brayden, we went into the lunchroom together to eat whatever terrible item was on the menu for the day.

Tuesday. 12:45 PM. The career fair.

Right after lunch was over, I went straight for the table with my spot. Dozens of mentors were already circling the room, talking with the students they had been paired with, and I couldn't wait to see what my career results were going to be.

Waiting patiently in my seat, I strained my eyes to see what careers my friends had gotten. It almost felt like Christmas morning, but without the presents, and without it being December, and without the eggnog, pecan pie, or spiced tea. Okay, so it was *nothing* like Christmas morning. It didn't matter how hard I looked for my friends though because there were too many people in the room to see anything past ten feet in front of me anyway.

I spun in my chair and opened the manila folder in front of me. My mentor was running a few minutes late, but maybe there was some information in the packet about what my career was.

Sure enough, I found a new slip of paper that had my test results on it!

All I had to do was skim the page and find out what kind of amazing life my future held. Video game designer? Comic book artist? Astronaut? Was it *at all* possible that my test paired me with a *ninja*?

Oh man! What if it *did*? I've been wondering why my mentor wasn't there yet, but… what if he was? What if it was a ninja, so good at ninja-ing that he was completely invisible somewhere out in the open?

My eyes skimmed faster down the page until I finally found

what I was looking for!

There it was – my name, Chase Cooper, with a bunch of dashes that trailed to the other side of the page, connecting with the career that I—

Chase Cooper --------------- Circus Clown

"Wait," I whispered. "*What?*"

Honka honka honka honka!

I let the paper fall from my hands. I watched it float through the air, past my black sneakers and across the floor tiles, until stopping at a pair of humongous red shoes.

"Hey there, kiddo!" a fully-grown man wearing makeup said. "We're gonna have a *honkin'* fun time!" His face became void of any emotion as he stared at me, honking his stinkin' clown horn like his life depended on it.

Honka honka!

I kid you not, every single person in that room stopped what they were doing to see what the most annoying sound in the world was.

"*Stop that!*" I hissed, tightening my lips. "*You're embarrassing me!*"

The clown tap-danced his oversized shoes toward me, which was frightening by itself, but tap dancing apparently wasn't enough. No, this clown also wanted to start blowing up one of those long balloons they make balloon animals out of.

So yeah, this *monster* was staring into my soul while twisting a long balloon into an animal and *also* tap dancing straight at me, and in a roomful of hundreds of spectators. The silence only made the squeaking balloons and metal taps that much worse.

I'm not gonna lie. I feared for my life.

"Okay. I was wrong before," I whispered. "*This* is how I actually die…"

The clown finally stopped tapping in front of me with a finale that extended an open palm out. "The name's *Miko*! My *friends* call me *Miko*, but *you* can call me *Miko*!"

At that point, everyone in the room returned to what they

were doing before the clown started acting out.

I slouched in my seat. "My name's Chase," I said. "You can call me Chase."

"Pleasure to make your acquaintance, Chase!" Miko said gleefully with his hand still outstretched toward me.

I made a fist, and bumped his open palm with it. Thankfully it was enough for him to set his hand down and take a seat next to me.

"Just my luck," I groaned. "I get paired with a *freak show.*"

Miko wagged his finger at me. "Now *that's* not vewy nice," he said in a goofy voice.

I shook my head, rubbing my eyes. "No, you're right. I'm sorry. I was just expecting something... different."

"Everyone does," Miko said with his silly voice slightly trailing away.

I leaned back, trying to make the best of the situation. "So like, this is your career then? Like, your *job* is to dress like a clown and stuff?"

"Yep," Miko said, honking his horn once.

Honka!

"Please stop," I said flatly. "So like, why? Why be a clown? Did you fail out of college or something?"

"Actually," Miko said, using his real voice, which was much deeper than I expected. "I had to *go* to college to do what I'm doing."

I paused. "What?"

"Yep," Miko continued. "I went to school for theater, and actually *chose* this career. I guess I'm just one of those guys who never really grew up, y'know? I just grew *older.*"

I blinked, only half-listening to what the clown was saying. I was too busy imagining a real ninja hiding somewhere in the cafeteria. "Don't you regret it?" I asked.

Miko stared at my eyes for a moment. "As a matter of fact, *no*, I *don't* regret it. I gotta say," he started wagging his finger at me again, "you're a little bit of an insensitive twerp, aren't you?"

I fell silent, unsure of what to say after getting burned by a clown.

The clown continued. "Hey, man. I'm just dishin' out the same stuff you're cookin', am I right?" He started honking his insanely loud horn at my face again. He knew it was embarrassing me, but *that's* why he was doing it.

Honka honka honka honka!

I stood from the table and started walking away, but Miko jumped up too. He tossed the balloon animal in the air and started patting upward at it with both palms. And then, as loudly as possible, he said, *"Hey, Chase! Don't let the balloon touch the ground! Wha-hoo!"*

I didn't know if anyone was even paying attention, but I'd never felt more embarrassed in my life. "Just leave me alone, okay? Go back to the table and wait until the end of the day, alright?"

Miko let the balloon drift to the ground. "Whatever you say, boss. I get paid to be here whether I'm mentoring or not." He turned and sat at the spot with my manila folder.

I scurried across the room like a mouse, feeling mortified

that Miko had made such a scene. If I could only find my friends in the crowded cafeteria, then I felt like I could begin to relax a little.

Nearing Brayden's table, I heard Zoe's voice sift through the crowd. "So *what's* his job?" she asked.

When I made it to their table, I saw what my friends were talking about. Brayden was sitting next to some guy wearing a giant wolf costume. At least I wasn't the only one paired with a strange career.

Brayden answered Zoe's question. "Wearing a wolf costume."

"How'd you manage to get that?" Faith asked. "What'd you say on your test?"

Brayden paused. "I was trying to manipulate the test so I'd get paired with a werewolf *hunter*…"

"But instead you got a guy in a wolf costume?" Zoe asked. "*How's that even a career?*"

"Hey!" The guy in the costume snipped. "*I* didn't choose to wear this wolf costume! This wolf costume chose *me*!"

"Could be worse, dude," I said. "At least you're not paired with a *clown*." I glanced over my shoulder at Miko. He was seated at my table, still wearing that creepy grin across his face. I felt a chill run down my spine.

Gavin was sitting on the other side of the table, speaking with his mentor, who looked like he was dressed for something sporty. "I'm not saying ya shouldn't be here, I'm just sayin' that maybe there was a mistake with my test! I was just expectin' to get some sort of soil job," Gavin said. "Y'see, my daddy was a soil man, just like *his* daddy before that, and his *daddy's* daddy before that! I come from a long line of soil men… Men proud of soilin' themselves."

"There's gotta be a better way of saying that," Zoe groaned, mortified.

"Sorry, dude," Gavin's mentor said. "Your test results don't lie. You got stuck with a rock climber."

"You mean you rock climb professionally?" Gavin asked.

Gavin's mentor nodded. "Yessir, been doin' it since I was a tiny kid."

"I didn't even know that rock climbing was a career," I said.

The man gave me a half smile. "Technically, it's *not*. I

mean, there are some people out there *killin'* it with their climbing skills, and those are the guys who are sponsored by soda companies and stuff. *Those* guys can call it a career."

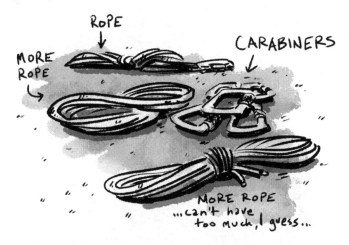

RoPE

MORE RoPE

CARABINERS

MORE RoPE
...can't have too much, I guess...

On the table in front of him were a few of his climbing tools. There were bundles of rope and a bunch of carabiners. You know, those metal circle things that keep rock climbers from falling off the side of a mountain, or the little circle thing that hipsters use as a keychain.

"So you wouldn't say rock climbing is your job?" Gavin asked, confused.

The man leaned forward with his "serious" face and stared deep into Gavin's eyes. "Rock climbing is my way of *life*, brother. It's my *reason* for *living*. It's the *blood* in my veins."

Gavin didn't even try to argue. "Okay then, I guess I can respect that."

From the corner of my eye, I saw Wyatt, but I knew it was because he *wanted* me to see him.

"I'll be right back, guys," I said taking a few steps.

Faith stood from the table. "Wait, where are you going?"

"I, uh, have to go to the bathroom!" I said. "Okay? BRB!"

Faith sat back down and kept talking to Zoe, Brayden, and Gavin. I didn't like keeping secrets from them, but if they knew I was working with Wyatt, they'd probably beat me up themselves.

On the other side of the room, I met with Wyatt, but had to make it look like I *wasn't* talking to him. He was sitting at one table, facing the west wall, so I took a seat at the table behind him, facing the east wall.

Naomi plopped herself down in the chair across from me. "What do you think you're doing?" she asked.

I scanned the room to see if anyone had noticed us. There was way too much happening for anyone to see anything though. "Nothing, alright?" I said. "I got this under control."

"Yeah," Wyatt said from behind me, still facing the opposite direction. "Beat it, will ya?"

Naomi leaned over and stared past me. "*Really?* You're doing this?"

"We're not doing anything wrong," I said. "Wyatt's helping me catch the bandit!"

Naomi shook her head. "Nuh-uh, not alone."

"C'mon, Naomi," I pleaded. "This isn't something you want to get mixed up in."

"But *you* do?" she retorted.

I nodded at her. "Touché," I said. "But seriously, it's something we can take care of ourselves."

Naomi folded her hands and looked at me like I was a child. "I'm not going anywhere. You two are going to play nicely, and *I'm* going to be the one to make sure of it."

Wyatt shook his head, growling out of frustration. "She's fine! Whatever! Just keep out of our way, and you can tag along, alright?"

"Deal," Naomi said with satisfied smile.

Just then I saw Sebastian enter the cafeteria with Principal Davis trailing behind him. The president made a couple gestures as he spoke to the principal, pointing toward the back corner of the cafeteria. Principal Davis laughed at something, and then nodded his head.

"What's *that* all about?" I asked.

Wyatt peeked over his shoulder. "Oh, remember how I said Principal Davis *loves* the fact that Sebastian has created a mini business during the career week?"

"Right," I said.

"Well, he loves it so much that he's allowing Sebastian to sell them in The Pit," Wyatt said. "They hope to have The Pit fully stocked by Friday."

"No way," Naomi said. "Good for Sebastian, I guess. He seems to be a really successful kid, doesn't he?"

"He just knows the right people," Wyatt said. "In this school, it's all about who you know."

"Those little block erasers are made by Sebastian?" Naomi asked. "Heads are nearly exploding over those little things."

Wyatt sighed. "Listen, we don't have much time, and it's going to start looking strange if anyone sees us talking to ourselves so let's make this quick, shall we?"

"What's the plan?" I asked.

"Tomorrow morning," Wyatt said. "Be here at 6:30 sharp, and bring a pack of gum."

"*6:30?*" I said, "But I don't even wake up until 7:25!"

"School starts at 7:45 though," Naomi said. "That gives you less than twenty minutes to get dressed and get to school on time."

"Correct," I said, pointing two fingers at her.

Naomi frowned. "Your mother must *hate* you in the mornings."

"Correct again!" I said, pointing my fingers a second time. I turned my head slightly so Wyatt could hear me. "Is there a little wiggle room in this schedule of yours? Like, maybe we can just meet after homeroom or something?"

Wyatt didn't answer.

When I looked over my shoulder, he wasn't there anymore. "Did you see him leave?" I asked Naomi.

She shook her head. "Say whatever you want about that kid, but there's no denying he's got skills when it comes to being a ninja."

For some reason, my gut twisted. I wasn't sure why, but the way Wyatt was able to disappear like that made me uncomfortable, and I found myself hoping that teaming up with him *wasn't* the biggest mistake of my life.

Naomi looked over her shoulder, watching Sebastian across the room. "Do you think the rumors are true?"

I had no idea what she was talking about. "Huh?" I grunted like an ape. "What rumors?"

"Y'know," she said, lowering her voice. "The rumors about the *Scavengers*. Do you think there's any truth to their existence?"

I leaned back, confused. "*What* are you talking about?"

Naomi looked at me, slightly surprised. "You *haven't* heard about them? How long have you been going to school here?"

To avoid feeling dumb, I spoke again. "Isn't a scavenger, like, an animal that feeds on things that are already dead?"

Naomi nodded, and then kept looking over both her shoulders like she was paranoid someone was there. "Yeah," she said. "But it also refers to people who collect stuff that others throw away."

I was beginning to feel a bit paranoid too. "What about them? Is there a group of kids around here like that?"

Naomi shrugged her shoulders. "Nobody knows for sure," she said. "But nobody ever talks about it either."

"Why not?"

Naomi paused. "Because the rumor is that the Scavengers are the ones who really control what's going on at Buchanan. They're the ones in charge. Supposedly Sebastian is one of them, but it's never been proven."

"Does everyone know about this rumor?" I asked.

"No," Naomi said. "But I figured that maybe you'd have at least heard about it since, y'know, you're the leader of a secret ninja clan."

Great. As if the red ninja clan wasn't enough for me to worry about, now I've got another secret club that's apparently *so secret* that almost nobody even knows that they even exist. If *this* was how sixth grade was going to be, then I didn't even want to *think* about what horrors *seventh* grade possibly held.

Wednesday. 6:25 AM. The hallways.

I got my mom to drop me off a few minutes before Wyatt wanted me to meet him. Getting to school by 6:30 meant waking up at the butt-crack of dawn, when the sun has barely risen. You ever wake up before the sun does? It's a really weird and confusing feeling.

Once I was in the lobby of Buchanan, I took a left turn and started down the hall. Principal Davis was already in his office typing away on his computer. Most of the other office staff were doing the same.

The school was so quiet that I could hear the balls bouncing in the gym from the basketball team practicing. Every now and again, the sound of squeaking tennis shoes was added to the mix.

There was something pleasant about how quiet and empty the corridors were. I think my dad would use the word "*tranquil*" to describe it – it means *peaceful*. Metal lockers loomed silently over me as I walked between them. I could even hear my shoes squish into the carpet with each step I took.

It was a really strange feeling to be in the building before anyone else was. I felt... *free*. Whenever I walk these halls, I always make sure I don't accidently shoulder bump someone, or I have to walk at a turtle's pace because a group of girls are staring at their cell phones and texting each other. But this morning, I could run as fast as I wanted without having to worry about anyone else.

In fact, that's exactly what I did.

Clutching my book bag straps, I cinched them tighter, and took off like a fox. The open hallway in front of me was practically begging me to sprint down it.

Cold air streamed past my face as I pushed myself harder to make it to the end of the corridor. The lockers on both sides of me became a blur of different colors, and for a second I imagined myself traveling back in time to when I first started at Buchanan.

I remember the first time stepping into the humongous lobby out front, and the sense of fear and excitement that came over me at the same time. I didn't recognize a single person in the crowd that day, but I also can't remember anyone's face. I wonder if Faith or Brayden were there too, and if they were, did they notice the new kid?

The end of the hall was coming up fast, but it connected with another hallway that I could easily turn in. I figure a couple laps in the morning would probably be a good way to jolt my system awake so instead of slowing down, I sped up.

Big mistake.

Just as I turned the corner, I felt a sharp pain in my knees. I felt the floor disappear from under my feet and watched as the entire hallway flipped upside-down until I suddenly slammed into the wall. Maybe zooming around corners without looking both ways was a bad idea.

I heard what sounded like a cardboard box fall to the ground, and then saw several colorful little bricks bounce around me.

"What's the *matter* with you?" an angry boy shouted at me, holding one of his shins. "You about busted my leg!"

I sat up and leaned against the wall. "Sorry about that," I said as I rubbed my eyes.

The little bricks around me were Sebastian's rubber block erasers that he had been selling in the school. Tons of them were scattered down the hall from my unfortunate accident with the other student. "Really, I'm—," I stopped midsentence when I realized who was on the floor next to me.

It was Jake, leader of the wolf pack.

Oh yeah, and he's also a member of Wyatt's red ninja clan. I could see the red bracelet around his wrist.

I didn't want any trouble, so I scooped up a few of the block erasers and held them out to Jake.

He batted my hand away, knocking the block erasers out of it. "Keep your meat hooks off of those! You want one, you can buy one from The Pit!"

I was surprised. "So they're letting him sell these through The Pit for sure?" I asked.

Jake rolled his eyes at me as he tossed the tiny colored bricks back into the box. "Uh, duh, why would I tell you to buy one there? Try using your brain sometime, you'll find it helps conversations move forward rather than in circles."

I knew if I kept talking, it was only going to make things worse, so I stayed quiet. I'd probably toss an insult, and then he'd toss one back, and it would keep going like that until something in his head snapped and he came at me like a banshee. Sometimes it *is* better to say nothing.

Jake dumped the rest of the erasers back into the box, and hoisted it up. With one last dirty look, he continued his way toward the lobby.

Sebastian must have been making a fortune in those block erasers, especially if he's got a few people working for him. First it was Wyatt who needed to deliver a box of erasers to the front offices, and now Jake was carrying a second box.

I felt a cold breeze on my back, and heard the side door to the school seal itself shut.

"Good morning," Naomi's voice said from behind.

I turned and saw her walking toward me, both hands pushed into the front pouch of her hoodie. "Whaddup," I replied.

"See Wyatt anywhere yet?" Naomi asked, peeking down the hall.

I shook my head. "Nuh-uh, but he also didn't say where to meet him. He just kinda *vanished*."

"Or maybe I've been here the entire time," came an eerie voice from one of the classrooms in the hall. The door was cracked about an inch wide, with an eyeball pressed against the opening.

"Do you *live* here?" Naomi asked sarcastically.

The door swung open, and Wyatt stepped into the hallway. "Maybe," Wyatt said grinning. "Maybe not. The key to being a good ninja is being mysterious."

Naomi curled her lip. "How long have you been hiding in that classroom? Couple minutes? An hour? Did you sneak in there when you saw Chase and me talking? That would mean that you had to sneak into the room from the other side and then tip toe in the darkness until you made it to the door, which *then* means you had to silently unlock the latch so we wouldn't hear it, *all* so you could be creepy and say, '*maybe I've been here the whole time.*' Dude, seriously? If you're doing *all* that just so you can look cool, then you need to re-evaluate how you spend your time."

Wyatt's grin faded. "Maybe," he hissed, probably because he couldn't think of a good comeback. "Maybe not."

Naomi stuck her tongue out, scrunching her face to mock him. "*Maybe. Maybe not,*" she said in a little kid's voice.

Wyatt took a step toward her, but I stepped in the way. "Can we just get to the part about catching the bandit? It's already 7:00, and we're just wasting time now."

The muscles in Wyatt's jaw twitched. "Agreed," he said. "Did you bring a pack of gum?"

I pulled out a rectangular pack of cinnamon gum from my pocket. My mom let me take one of her packs – she's got a million of them in a junk drawer that *reeks* of cinnamon.

"Excellent," Wyatt wheezed as he tapped his fingers together. "We're going to set a trap for the bandit this morning, and use your gum as bait."

I was confused, but curious. "Like, we're gonna tie a string to it or something? We're gonna go fishing for the bandit? Bandit fishing?" My jaw dropped, excited. "Oh, dibs! Band name! Called it! You can't use Bandit Fishing as a band name!"

Wyatt stared at me. "No," he said, annoyed. "We're not *tying a string* to this thing. We're just gonna set it down and watch it until someone nabs it."

I folded my arms, and grumbled. "I liked the *fishing* idea better."

"But what do we do when we find the bandit?" Naomi asked. "Just run after him or something?"

Another brilliant idea came to my mind. "Oh," I said, excited. "Once we figure out who the bandit is, we could find them during lunch! And then what we can do is hide in the ceiling right above them until they open their milk carton. Once their milk carton is open, we'll lower a thread down into his drink, and then send a single drop of truth serum down the thread until it drips into their milk, effectively tainting their beverage. After that, we'll confront the bandit in front of Principal Davis, and because of the truth serum, he'll spill his guts. Boom. Day saved *again* by the super handsome Chase Cooper. You lose, bandit, but *thanks* for playing."

Naomi and Wyatt looked at me in disbelief.

"Sweet idea, right?" I asked, smiling smugly.

Naomi held her hand out and extended her index finger. "One – hanging out in the ceiling of the cafeteria is probably asking for broken bones." She put up a second finger. "Two – even *if* truth serum was a real thing, we don't have access to it." A third finger lifted on her hand. "Three – it would be *way* easier to just nab this crook instead of the plan you just came up with." Naomi's pinky finger was the last to extend. "And four – I'm concerned that if I wasn't here to put a stop to your *bonkers* plan, you and Wyatt would *probably* try to actually carry it out!"

"I think we'd stop once we couldn't get our hands on the truth serum," Wyatt said.

I folded my arms and glanced to the side. "Fine," I said. "I guess we'll just try to catch the kid."

"Good," Naomi said. "Let's get started then, shall we?"

Wednesday. 7:30 AM. The hallways.

Since the bandit was able to strike anywhere at anytime, we figured there wasn't a *bad* place to set our trap. After a short discussion, we chose the short hallway that wrapped around the front offices. It was just out of the way so that we could remain hidden, but in an area where traffic was still pretty thick. It was perfect.

"Okay, one more time," I said, staring into the bottom of the garbage can. "We put the gum on that water fountain over there while I hide in this nasty rubber container over here, and when the bandit strikes, I jump out and catch him?"

We were behind the door to the janitor's closet, safely hidden from other students. Their shadows danced in the small opening at the bottom of the door.

Wyatt held his palms out. "What's so difficult about that plan? Why do you keep repeating it like that?"

"It's just, I mean," I said, trying to find the words. "There's *gotta* be a more ninja way to do this."

"What's more ninja than hiding in a garbage can?" Wyatt asked.

Naomi pressed her lips together and pointed at Wyatt. "He's got a point."

"Really?" I whined. "You agree with *him*?"

"Honestly, I just want to see you sit in that garbage can," Naomi giggled.

"I'm not even wearing my ninja mask," I said.

Wyatt raised an eyebrow. "Just because you're not wearing your ninja mask doesn't mean you're *not* a ninja."

He made a good point.

"Now get in there, tiger," Wyatt smirked.

Returning my attention to the bottom of the gray barrel, I saw all kinds of half-eaten nasty food, and felt sorry for the janitors at the school. People could at least empty their soda cans before tossing them out!

I imagined, for a moment, the rise of the garbage cans in the future. One day, they'll come to life and seek vengeance for all the gunk that people stuffed into them. Just remember this on the day when it happens and garbage cans begin devouring the human race because they're fed up – that I, Chase Cooper, *totally* called it.

I shut my eyes and mustered up some courage I had been saving for just such an occasion. "*So gross*," I whispered as I set my feet into the bottom of the garbage can. I gripped the sides so I wouldn't slip on whatever mushy nastiness awaited me in the pit of the barrel.

Finally, I was completely crouched and tucked away like a ninja… hiding in a garbage can. Wyatt gently set the lid on top, but not without laughing at my expense.

I felt the can begin to roll along the floor as Naomi and Wyatt wheeled me across the hall, over to where out trap had been set by the water fountains.

Now all I had to do was wait.

Pushing up on the lid, I got to a point where I could see my pack of gum without giving away my position. Kids kept passing the bait, not even noticing it was there. A couple kids even took sips from the fountains, but left the cinnamon gum alone!

At that point, I was starting to feel claustrophobic. The inside of the rubber barrel was getting hotter, and the stink of bananas and fish was overwhelming. At least if I needed to barf, I was already in the spot to do it.

And then it happened. I saw a hand reach out toward the pack of gum. I had to wait until the student had the gum in his hands before jumping out because they had to be caught red handed – with the pack of my gum in their possession.

The large hand touched the gum, and then the student pinched it with his fingers, raising it into the air. We got him! We got the bandit!

Who's throwing fish away in the hallway garbage???

Instantly, I exploded out of the garbage and grabbed the student's arm! "*Ah-ha!*" I shouted, pointing my finger at the bandit's guilty face. "*Caught youuuuuuuuuuuuuuuuu...*" I trailed off the second I realized it was Principal Davis's arm in my hand.

The principal stared at my finger. "*What's the meaning of this?*"

"Heh," I laughed nervously, unable to release the principal's hand from my death-grip. "I um, that's uh, it's just sommmmme.... ummm…"

"First of all," the principal said, pulling his hand away from me. "You're *not* allowed to have gum, so I'm *taking* this! Second of all, hiding at the bottom of garbage cans is probably *never* a good idea! And lastly? It looks like you've set a trap here."

I wasn't sure what to say, so my brain automatically made me smile, totally making me look like a guilty nutcase.

"You're *not* setting traps in the school, are you, Chase?" Principal Davis asked with a groan.

70

Suddenly, Wyatt burst from the door across the hall. "Of course he's not setting a trap! He's merely helping me with a social experiment!"

The principal raised his eyebrows. "Oh really?" he asked, suspicious.

To be fair, what we were doing *could* be considered a social experiment. I mean, we're baiting a thief to come out of hiding, hoping that the temptation was enough to trigger their evil desire.

Wyatt responded quickly. "Yes! We wanted to see if the person who took this gum would take it to the lost and found!"

The principal's face didn't move. He looked at Wyatt, and then glanced at the pack of gum. "Well, this *experiment* is over. You can't have gum anyway so it wouldn't matter if they took it to the lost and found. They'd have just thrown it away."

"Ah," Wyatt said, smiling. "Good to know. Thank you, sir. Have a great day."

The principal squeezed the pack of gum in his hands and disappeared around the corner.

"Quick thinking," Naomi said, stepping out of the room. She looked up at the clock on the wall. "Whoops, gonna be late. We better get going."

Wyatt helped me out of the garbage can. "It's alright," He said. "We'll have to catch the bandit later today."

I nodded, picking tiny pieces of garbage off my clothing. "Right," I said. "As long as *you're* in the garbage can next time."

Wednesday. 7:47 AM. Homeroom.

I had to sneak into my homeroom since I was a little late. It took me a couple extra minutes to wipe my shoes off on the edge of the garbage can. All that trouble, and for nothing!

At the desk in front of me, Zoe sniffed at the air. "*Nasty*! What *is* that?"

I didn't say anything, hoping that maybe she was smelling something *other* than me.

My cousin turned around, disgusted. "Ew, dude! Is that *you*? *What's all over your clothes?*"

"I was hiding in a garbage can—" I started to say.

"Because that's how *normal* kids start their day," Zoe interrupted. "I'm not sure that hanging out with Wyatt is working out for you."

I was shocked. "How... how did you know?"

"How'd we know you and Wyatt are buddy-buddy now?" Brayden asked, leaning closer. "C'mon, man. We're not dumb. It's obvious. Plus Naomi said something to me yesterday about it."

I closed my fist. "*Naomi!*"

"Um, no," Zoe said. "You're not allowed to be upset with her. She was just telling us because she was concerned about you."

"There's nothing to be concerned about though!" I said, leaning back in my seat. Zoe was right; the putrid smell of garbage was lingering on me.

"There's not?" Zoe asked. "Let's see, you're late to class and you stink like a dead skunk that came back to life and then

72

died again. This is about all that gum that was stolen, isn't it?"

I didn't intentionally repeat Wyatt's words, but they came out anyway. "Maybe," I said. "Maybe not."

"Do I need to remind you that Wyatt and Sebastian are working together?" Zoe snipped. "So while you're out saving the school from a gum bandit, *those* two are still up to something. And whatever it is probably ain't good!"

I thought about it for a moment. "What if this is my chance to do something good *without* having to deal with costumed ninjas? Maybe my good influence can rub off on Wyatt. If that's the case, then isn't it worth a shot?"

Zoe sighed, and looked me right in the eye. "I get it," she said. "You're all about honor and all that. But I just don't want you to get in any kind of trouble. It's always easier to get dragged down by someone than it is to pull them up."

After that, Zoe turned around for the rest of homeroom. She was right, and I knew she was, but she didn't seem to understand that all I wanted to do was to find the gum bandit. At this point, it almost felt like an obsession.

I could overhear some conversations in class about how more gum had been stolen, so I knew the bandit was still out there. He just didn't happen to steal the gum we had tried to lure him with.

No matter though, because it was still early, and there was plenty of time left in the day.

Wednesday. 11:40 AM. Lunch.

I stood outside the cafeteria, rolling the packet of gum in the palms of my hand. As students passed me to get in line for lunch, I watched their eyes to see if they would look at the bait in my hand. Too bad *every single kid* looked – kinda makes it hard to single anyone out as the bandit.

"I guess we're trying this again?" Naomi asked as she approached. She was a good ninja. A devoted ninja. I knew I could count on her.

I nodded. "If Wyatt ever shows up."

"Why wait for him?" Naomi asked. "If he's late, it's his fault. You don't need him for any of this."

She was right. "Okay," I said. "Let's do this."

"Where do we start?" Naomi asked, putting her hands on her hips and watching the students in line.

I pulled a piece of thread from my book bag. "During art class, I managed to get a piece of string. I say we tie one end to the gum, and the other end to my bag, and just wait. No garbage cans and no stinky mess. We don't even have to pay attention to the pack of gum! When the bandit takes it, the string will catch our attention!"

"*Bandit fishing*," Naomi said.

"Bandit fishing," I repeated, smiling.

Naomi helped me tie the string around the cinnamon gum pack while I secured the other end to one of the zippers on my bag. After the trap was set, we entered the cafeteria, but made sure to stay near the opening. If the bandit *were* to take the bait, the first thing he'd do would be run out of the cafeteria, so we wanted to make sure it would be easy to follow him out the doors.

I stuck the gum in the small pocket on the side of my book bag, just enough so that the end was visible. It was just screaming to get stolen. I took a seat on the bench by the door. Naomi took the spot next to me.

"The other ninjas love the new hideout," Naomi said, making conversation. "But you've only been there once this week."

Naomi was talking about the unused wrestling room I had stumbled upon a week ago. I was chasing Hotcakes, the penguin, through the school and ended up in that room. Part of me thinks Hotcakes *wanted* to show it to me. Since the room was unused, Coach Cooper said I was allowed to use it for a martial arts club. My ninja clan would have a legit place to train that would still be hidden from the rest of the school. It was perfect.

"I know I should be training with them," I replied, "but this situation has taken more attention from me than I wanted."

Naomi nodded. "You should still try to make time for them. I mean, they're not only part of your ninja clan, but they're your friends too."

"I know, I know," I whispered, feeling guilty. The truth was that I *wanted* to train with them. A sixth grade ninja who doesn't train is just a sixth grade *kid*.

At that moment, the zipper on my book bag flipped. I spun around, trying to get a look at the pack of gum, but it wasn't there anymore.

"Did you see who took it?" I asked, frantically jumping from the bench. "It happened so quast that I didn't see anything!"

"No!" Naomi said. "I was watching the cafeteria! Wait... what? What's *quast* mean?"

I felt like a dimwit. "I meant to say *'quick,'* but at the last second tried to say *'fast.'* So it just came out as *'quast.'"*

"Nice," Naomi smiled.

My bag jerked to the left, pulling me along with it. The string was still attached to the gum! I plucked at the tight piece of thread, making the same sound as a guitar string. Following it with my eyes, I saw that it was getting tugged toward the staff entrance of the kitchen, and *not* back into the lobby like Naomi and I had assumed it would.

"Come on!" I said, racing along the wall, dodging students who were trying to find a seat with their food.

Naomi dashed past me like a bullet. She pulled the door to the kitchen open for me and we stepped through.

Inside the kitchen was a hot mess of steam and food. The cooks were too busy moving tubs of spaghetti sauce back and forth to notice the two kids that had just walked through the door.

"This is why the bandit chose this exit," I said. "Everyone's too distracted to see anything!"

"And the noise level is through the roof!" Naomi added, nearly shouting.

She was right. It was hard to hear *anything* over the voices of the cooks and the clanging pots and pans.

Naomi stepped forward and touched her finger to the string on my bag. It was still pulled tight, but not as tight as before. There was a little slack, which meant that the bandit had stopped running.

I followed Naomi as she jogged through the kitchen, past the adults who were busy at their jobs. The smell of pasta and mashed potatoes was thick in the air as we turned the corner.

We were in the back of the kitchen now, where all the dry food was stored. Massive containers of mayonnaise, ketchup, and mustard were stacked on shelves across the entire room. Huge pallets of buns were set at the center and at the back of the room was another exit.

The string on my bag was completely loose at that point. The bandit had either stopped moving completely or had cut the string off. I was beginning to doubt we'd find him back there.

The white thread led from the zipper on my book bag to the floor, where it weaved around the pallet of buns and disappeared under the door at the back of the room.

"Great," I said, defeated. "He's long gone by now."

Naomi stepped forward. "Maybe not," she said, pointing at the string sticking out from under the door.

It was moving, but only slightly.

My heart started racing. "He's still messing with the gum!" I said. "The bandit is right on the other side of this door!"

Naomi grabbed the handle of the door and smiled at me. "Are you ready for this?"

I swallowed hard, and then took a deep breath. "Do it."

Pushing the handle down, Naomi unlatched the handle and pulled the door open with all her strength.

I wasn't sure what I was expecting to see. In my head the entire time, I had always thought the bandit would look like a small mouse, dressed in blue jeans, a white t-shirt, and a leather coat, with greased black hair and a stupid grin. I think I saw a movie like that once.

Instead, of seeing the silly cartoon character from my head, I saw the end of the piece of string laying on the ground. My packet of gum had been cut off the string.

All the hope and excitement that had built up inside me suddenly vanished, and I was left with an empty feeling.

"We weren't fast enough," I said. "We *had* him, but we just weren't *fast* enough!"

Naomi was by my side, but she didn't say anything.

"If we could've only been—"

Naomi nudged me with her elbow. "Chase? You might wanna turn around now."

Great. That was never a good thing to hear.

I looked over my shoulder to see what was spooking Naomi. Across the room, were three red ninjas – they always travel in packs of three.

"Lookie what we got here," the ninja at the front sneered. "A couple of kiddos who have lost their way."

I narrowed my eyes. "Jake?"

The ninja grabbed the bottom of his mask by his chin and ripped it off. His black hair flopped all over the place before it fell on his forehead.

It *was* Jake, and the two red ninjas behind him were probably members of his wolf pack.

Jake held his fist out at me. "You *hurt* my leg in the hallway this morning, and for *that*, you will *pay.*"

"That's a little extreme, isn't it?" Naomi asked.

"Not for a star football player!" one of the red ninjas behind Jake said. "This guy is *needed* for our team, and you injured him!"

"It was an accident, and I said I was sorry!" I shouted.

"That doesn't mean you don't get a consequence!" Jake said. He punched his fist into the palm of his hand. "Get them!"

I wasn't sure what to do. The room was small, and there wasn't much I could use to help me defend myself, except for the buns at the center of the room.

Part of a ninja's training involves learning how to use their surroundings to their advantage. A ninja has to be aware of everything around them at all times, so they can be prepared for anything, even if the only thing around them was a palette of bread buns.

"Bun attack!" I shouted, grabbing handfuls of the small round loaves of bread.

Chucking them across the room, I managed to get both of the red ninjas who were coming toward me. They flinched, stepping back toward Jake.

"He's throwing *bread* at you!" Jake shouted angrily.

Naomi grabbed the handle of the door behind us and pulled as hard as she could, but the door didn't budge. "It's jammed! The only way out is *through* them!"

"Of course it is!" I replied. "Because that's my luck, isn't it? James Buchanan is trying to ruin my life by trapping me in a kitchen with red ninjas!"

"You need some serious help!" Naomi screamed, frustrated. Grabbing a handful of buns, she joined me, swinging her arm around like she was pitching a softball. "These things are as soft as marshmallows!"

The two red ninjas stuck their chests out and started marching toward Naomi and me. They knew the door behind us was stuck so they weren't in any hurry to beat the living tar out of us.

"It's been an honor to serve with you, sir," Naomi said, way more serious than I think she meant to.

"We're not out of the game yet!" I said, balling one of the rolls into a tight wad of bread. "Check *this* out!"

I threw it at one of the red ninjas as hard as I could. The ball of bread zoomed through the air so fast that it made a "*fsssshhhh*" sound. Time seemed to stand still as the bun drew closer and closer to the red ninja's face. I could see the fear in his eyes. He wanted to panic, but his brain wasn't fast enough to make his body respond.

Closer and closer until... it sailed *over* his head.

Naomi slapped her forehead. "This is how *I* die."

I chuckled since I've had that same exact thought a couple times earlier in the week. Naomi and I actually had a lot in common – too bad I discovered that at the worst possible time.

The two red ninjas approached with their fists in the air. Naomi took a step back, planting her foot firmly in the ground. I did the same, waiting for the attack.

Suddenly, the jammed door burst open from behind us, flooding the room with sunlight. The two ninjas stumbled about, unable to see anything. They covered their faces, shielding their eyes from the light.

A figure stood tall in the doorway as sunlight bathed over it. The light was so bright that it was impossible to see the figure's face.

"The white ninja?" Naomi whispered, squinting her eyes.

"I don't know," I said, realizing the person in the door was wearing a goofy looking outfit. It was still difficult to see, but it was obvious that the figure was wearing some sort of one-piece costume. The man's outline looked almost the same as a clown's outfit. Was Miko standing in the doorway?

"Leave them alone!" the shadowed figured commanded.

"Miko, is that you?" I asked, squinting. "Are you wearing your clown outfit?"

"Clowns!" Jake said quickly. "No! No clowns! *No clowns!*"

The two red ninjas looked at each other confused.

"You know I have a fear of clowns!" Jake shouted as he tripped over his feet. "I *hate* clowns! They're unnatural! *Why would anyone ever want to paint their face like that? Why?*"

The two red ninjas ran to the leader of the wolf pack and helped him to his feet.

"Ninjas!" Jake shouted. "Vanish!"

One of the ninjas pulled out a sack filled with chalk dust and slammed it on the ground. When the dust had started clearing, all three red ninjas were gone.

I spun around, ready to confront whoever was standing in the door. "Miko?" I asked again cautiously.

80

The figure stepped into the kitchen and shut the door behind him. Naomi's jaw about hit the floor when she saw his face.

It was Wyatt, and he was wearing overalls.

"No way," I said to myself. Did Wyatt really just save the day? Had he seriously turned over a new leaf? Like, for real?

Wyatt acted like it wasn't a big deal. "That was crazy, huh? Did you ever get that box of erasers to the front office like I asked you to do?"

I shook the disbelief from my head because even though Wyatt might've saved us, it still didn't change the fact that members of *his* red ninja clan were trying to hurt us. "Those were *your* ninjas!" I said, ignoring his question about the box of erasers.

Wyatt nodded, setting his hands on his hips like he was disappointed. "I know, I know. What a bunch of jerks, right?"

I stared at Wyatt for a moment, my mind completely blown. *"Are you kidding me?"*

"What?" Wyatt said, annoyed.

"Those guys are on *your* team!"

Scratching the back of his head, Wyatt spoke. "Too bad they were wearing their masks or else we'd know who it was."

"It was Jake!" Naomi said. "Jake *didn't* have his mask on!"

"Jake?" Wyatt asked, looking a little more than confused as he walked across the room. "Man, I've had problems with that kid since... well, since he joined my clan."

Biting my lip, I stared toward the direction Jake and his wolf pack ran off in.

"Wait," Wyatt said suddenly. "You don't suppose..."

I glanced at Wyatt, waiting for him to finish.

"You don't think *he's* the one stealing all the gum, do you?"

I looked back at the exit and saw my string leading out the door. "No. He came in *after* we followed the bandit back here."

"You..." Wyatt said softly. "Followed the bandit back here? Did you *see* the bandit?"

Naomi stepped forward. "For all we know, the bandit is *you*. The gum was taken out the exit door, and the string was *also* detached out there! And then *who* happens to use that door to save us?"

Wyatt put his hands up. "I can tell you right now that I'm *not* the bandit. Remember? I was sitting with Chase the first day

81

the bandit even struck!"

I looked at Naomi, nodding.

She folded her arms and scowled at the floor.

"But," Wyatt continued. "Jake just happened to be back here after you lost the bandit? Doesn't that sound *too* coincidental? I mean, look around! Why would he hang out in the kitchen?"

"I don't know," Naomi said. "Why are *you* hanging out in the kitchen? And wearing those ridiculous overalls?"

Wyatt pulled the denim straps on his shoulders proudly. "I'm volunteering my time back here. I was out taking the trash to the dumpster before all this, which is why I was outside."

"Volunteering?" I asked.

"I'm the vice president now," Wyatt sighed. "I've got to do things like this in order to look good."

I chuckled.

Naomi pressed her lips together and looked at me. "He's got a point. Why *would* Jake and his wolf pack even be back here?"

It didn't make sense, that's for sure. Wyatt was right – Jake and his red ninjas had no reason to hang out in the kitchen at all so the fact that they suddenly appeared *right after* we lost the bandit was something to think about.

But if the red ninjas *were* the ones behind the theft, then that would mean Wyatt would *have* to have something to do with it, wouldn't it? How would the leader of the red ninjas *not* have a clue about what his clan was doing?

If Wyatt were in on it, then that would mean he was playing me, right? But how can Wyatt be in on it if *he's* the one who suggested it was *Jake* in the first place?

Seriously! It felt like my brain was crying! I was beginning to feel like all of this was a little too much to handle on my own. Naomi had been by my side the entire time, but even *she* warned me about getting involved in the first place.

Maybe my friends were right. Maybe I shouldn't have taken on this case when I did. No one else in the school seemed to care, so maybe I shouldn't either.

Wednesday. 12:40 PM. The career fair.

I sat at my seat in the cafeteria when the career fair started. All around me were other students laughing and having a good time with their mentors. Even Brayden looked like he was having a good time with the kid in the wolf costume.

Zoe was mixing glasses of lemonade with her mentor. Faith was looking at a laptop screen with hers. I swear, if I saw a ninja mentoring some other kid in this room, I was gonna lose it.

"Howdy, kiddo!" Miko said as he flopped his huge red feet toward me, each step slapping the ground like an oversized flapjack.

I tightened a smile, not even trying to make it look genuine. "S'up," I said while also using the international gesture for 'hello' by nodding my head upward, but only once, in the clown's general direction.

Miko took the spot next to me. After a moment, he spoke again, but using his normal voice. "So hey, there's this kid I keep seeing around here. His left calf muscle is bigger than his right one, and I mean like, *scary* big. Like that was the only part of his body that he decided to work out."

"Oh, you mean Brian?" I asked.

The clown stared at me. "Um, if *Brian* has a monster hiding in his left leg then yes, Brian. What's his deal?"

"He broke the right pedal off his bicycle at the beginning of the year," I explained. "He keeps saying he's gonna replace it, but I think he likes the attention. Plus he keeps going around telling everyone he's super ripped, even if it's only in the one calf."

"Seriously," Miko said, shaking his head. "If he kicked me with that leg, I'd probably have to go to the hospital."

I laughed.

Miko took notice that my guard was down. "Want to hear a joke?"

"Hit me," I said.

"Knock-knock," Miko said.

Wonderful. A classically boring knock-knock joke. "Who's there?" I asked.

"Banana."

"Banana who?"

Miko snickered, covering his nose. "Banana you glad I didn't say ban... wait, I messed that up. Let me start over. Knock knock."

It was easily the worst joke I'd ever heard, and the fact that he messed it up should've made it *less* funny, but it got me, and I LOL'd. It was actually kinda nice to take my mind off Jake, the wolf pack, and the Buchanan bandit.

The clown sighed and leaned back against the table. He pulled a soda can from one of his oversized pockets and popped it open, letting it fizz over a little. It was an orange soda, which happened to be my favorite out of all the sodas in the entire history of canned beverages.

"What's your deal?" I said out of the blue. "Did you lose a bet or something?"

Miko looked a little annoyed. "Why? Because I'm dressed like a clown?"

I nodded. "Yeah. Did your friends bet you wouldn't do this?"

"Surprisingly," Miko said, "all my friends are clowns too."

I let out a short laugh. "Yeah? That's something I'd like to see," I said sarcastically. "You should get *all* your clown buddies to perform on Friday. That'd be totes cool."

The clown raised his eyebrows. "But no, I didn't *lose* a bet. I *chose* this job."

"But why?" I asked, sitting forward. "That's what I don't understand! Why would you *choose* such a lame job?"

Miko paused. "Because I love doing it."

"Typical answer," I said.

"If you'd quit being such a thick toenail for a second, maybe you'd see that I was telling the truth," Miko said, upset.

"You love wearing too much makeup and an outfit that looks like you're just wearing a tent?" I joked.

"I love *performing,* and I love making people *laugh,*" Miko said. "I love see someone genuinely laugh until they cry. Making people happy, even if it's just for a second, is the reason why I do this. But more importantly, if I didn't love doing it, I'd be doing something else."

I stopped to think for moment. Miko was right, and I felt bad. "I'm sorry," I said. "I've just got a lot on my plate right now."

"Yeah?" Miko said. "What could a sixth grader possibly be stressing about?"

I looked Miko in the eye. "Just because I'm in sixth grade doesn't mean my life is all rainbows and gumdrops. Just 'cause I go to school all day and play video games all night doesn't mean I'm *not* dealing with some things."

It was Miko who apologized that time. "Sorry, man," he said softly. "You're right. Problems are problems, no matter who you are."

I nodded. "Thanks," I said, feeling embarrassed. "So this clown thing... you love doing it, huh?"

"Sure do," Miko said without missing a beat.

I sighed. "I can see that in you, I really can. I'm actually a little jealous that I can't make that kind of decision."

"What kind of decision?" Miko asked.

"Y'know, just to live life without caring what anyone else thinks," I said, gesturing to everyone in the room. "As a sixth grader, I feel like my entire life is sometimes controlled by what's cool and what's not."

"What you *think* is cool," Miko said, correcting me. "That's where the difference is, and it's a *huge* difference."

I looked at the clown, confused. "What do you mean?"

Miko sat quietly for a second, observing the other students. And then he answered. "Be inspired by the things you love – not by the things you *think* you should love."

"Huh?" I said.

Miko continued. "Like, I remember when I was your age, I

was really into comic books – superhero comics especially."

I nodded. "Right. Me too... me too."

"Well," Miko said. "I kind of got made fun of for it because I'd always have a stack of comics in my backpack. While other dudes were writing notes to girls, I had my face buried in the latest issue of my favorite comic."

I kept nodding. "What's that got to do with—"

"Can I finish?" Miko asked, a little annoyed.

"Sorry."

"Anyways, after a few times of getting made fun of because I read comics, I kind of took a little break from them. Nobody was ever really *mean* about it, but they still *said* things, y'know? Jokes about when I'd grow up and get a girlfriend or something."

I totally understood. "Even a tiny comment can ruin my day."

"Exactly!" Miko said. "All that happened was that someone shook their head at me and called me immature. That's *all* they said, but that was it for me. I stopped reading comics for many years because of that."

I sat forward, resting my elbows on my knees. "Man..."

"I know, right?" Miko said. "It took a few years before I realized that I really missed reading comics. Like, a lot."

"That's *lame* though," I said. "You shouldn't have stopped reading them in the first place if you loved them so much! Who *cares* what other people think? Comic books are harmless, and if they bring a little bit of joy to you, then read 'em! But that's not even talking about *just* comics! Like, you shouldn't be ashamed about *anything* you love, especially if... oh... I get it now."

Miko pointed his finger at me and smiled. "Bingo."

"Whoa," I whispered. "You just blew my mind."

Miko chuckled.

"I just wish it were that easy," I added, watching the kids in the cafeteria.

Miko sighed. "It never is."

Wednesday. 2:40 PM. After school.

I met Zoe outside the side doors of the school. Since we live pretty close to each other, her dad gives me a ride home too. She was sitting at a picnic table under the shade of a giant tree, already texting her friends on her phone.

"Whatcha doing?" I asked, setting my book bag on the table.

"Texting," Zoe replied. "Faith is coming over later tonight for dinner. Oh! Ask your parents if you can come too! It'll be fun!"

Zoe was my cousin. Her dad was my dad's brother. Every Sunday our families would get together for brunch, usually switching houses back and forth each week. Every now and again, we'd all hang out on a weeknight too so Zoe's invitation would probably be accepted.

"I'll ask," I said, staring top of the table, watching the shadows of leaves as they trembled in the breeze.

Zoe set her cell phone down and folded her hands. She wanted me to know I had her full attention. "What's the matter? Why are you so distracted?"

I didn't say anything.

"It's this thing with Wyatt, isn't it?"

Again, I didn't say anything.

"Look at how you're acting," Zoe said. "It's clearly affecting you."

"It's not *just* Wyatt," I said finally. "It's also the gum bandit. It's Jake and his wolf pack. It's all the homework I haven't done yet. It's Miko and his life lessons. It's whatever Sebastian is planning with Wyatt. It's Faith. It's Naomi. It's just… it's everything at the same time right now. *All of it.* The whole world seems to be resting on my shoulders."

"I think that maybe you're taking on too much this time," Zoe said. "I mean, I understand that you feel like you need to do something about the bandit, but really, I think it's Wyatt that's dragging you down the most out of all that stuff."

"I know," I admitted.

"It's not easy to hang around people like that," Zoe said. "At least it's not when you're the complete opposite of that person. Y'know? I used to have this friend here, I mean, she still goes to school here, but we hardly ever talk anymore. I think I've said maybe one word to her this entire year."

"What happened?" I asked.

"She fell in with the wrong crowd," Zoe said, shrugging her shoulders. "At first it was alright, but the more I hung out with her, the more I felt myself change a little bit. She was never really an overly negative person before, but after she started hanging out with some other kids, she suddenly became all drama. *Drama drama drama.* All she ever did was talk smack about pretty much everyone, and complain about everything. She just became so… *ugly* on the inside."

"What did you do?" I asked.

"I tried to stay friends with her," Zoe replied. "My parents said that she probably needed someone positive in her life, but after a little while, I just couldn't do it anymore. This one time she texted me to ask if I had been invited to someone's birthday party – I guess she saw a bunch of pictures posted online or something. When I told her I wasn't invited, her response was, 'Good, I just wanted to make sure I wasn't the only one. LOL.'"

"Wow," I said, floored.

"Yeah," Zoe said, nodding. "Seriously, I'm alright with not getting invited to parties. I get it. Sometimes they're just for a certain group of friends, or maybe even family, but that text made me feel like I was being *excluded* from something when I wasn't excluded at all. It made me *sick* inside. I sometimes wonder if she *wanted* me to feel bad so she wasn't alone."

Zoe's dad pulled up. He honked the horn twice and waved.

"Okay, you're right," I said, grabbing my book bag. "I'm done with Wyatt. It was a mistake that was making my stomach turn, and you just made me realize why."

Zoe didn't say anything, but she didn't have to. I could tell she was proud.

Instead, she punched me in the arm the way buddies do, but the thing about Zoe was that she liked to mix it up sometimes, and this time she threw a really hard punch. I winced, laughing the pain off and acting like it didn't hurt, but I'm pretty sure it was going to bruise.

Thursday. 7:40 AM. Before school.

The next morning was the same story – the gum bandit had struck again, and only the students of Buchanan knew it. If any of the teachers overheard conversations in the hallways, then *maybe* they were aware of the stealing spree, but if they *had* heard, they sure didn't show any signs of knowing.

Here's the weird thing though – if a stranger came and visited the school, they'd see almost everyone *chewing on gum.*

That's right. As I made my way through the students in the hallway, it was actually easier to count how many kids *weren't* chewing on gum. It was almost like there was *more* of it since the bandit started on Monday. It might've been possible that kids were so afraid of getting their gum stolen that they chewed on it instead of leaving it in their bags.

Suddenly, Wyatt appeared by my side. It's creepy how good he is at that.

"What's the plan for today?" he asked.

"What do you mean?" I replied.

"I mean, how are we gonna bust this bandit?"

"Oh, right. Look, I've been thinking a lot about it, and I think I'm just gonna give up on the whole thing."

Wyatt's face grew angry. "But you can't! Not when you're this close! I mean, not when *we're* this close!"

"How do you think we're close?" I asked.

"Jake!" Wyatt explained. "Jake was there in the kitchen yesterday! He *has* to be the bandit!"

"But if it's Jake, then maybe I *should* quit pressing the issue," I said. "Seems like he's playing the role of the new bully in school, and that's not exactly a show I'd like to be a part of."

"But if you *bust* him, then you can be the hero!" Wyatt said. "Again!"

I stopped in the middle of the hallway. "If it's so important to you, why don't *you* bust him?"

Wyatt stuttered an answer, but stopped immediately. He stepped closer to me and whispered as if he were telling a secret. "Because I'm the vice president, and that's enough attention for me. I've become happy being the guy who's 'behind the scenes' all the time. Y'know?"

"And here I thought you'd settle for nothing less than the 'lead actor,'" I said, suspicious.

Wyatt grinned, placing his hand on my shoulder and pushing me along. "Seriously," he said quietly. "I'm *trying* to be a better person, and I see this whole situation as my test. If I can help bust the bandit *and* make it so that *you're* the hero, then I feel like the universe will reward me for it. I think it's called karma."

"So you think if you do good things, then good things will happen to you?" I asked.

Wyatt nodded.

I sighed, still feeling unchanged about the situation. I brushed his hand off my shoulder, and continued to walk without him. "I'm out," I said confidently. "There's just something about all this that's making my skin crawl, and I just need to trust my instinct."

Wyatt didn't follow me. He remained perfectly still in the middle of the hallway, making it difficult for the other students to walk. I knew he was staring daggers at me, but I didn't care. I made my decision, and I was happy with it.

Thursday. 11:40 AM. Lunch.

After thinking about it all morning, I was feeling great about the decision to leave the bandit behind. It was more trouble than it was worth, and the whole thing would blow over anyway. Everyone would forget that the bandit even existed after the week was over.

As I walked into the cafeteria, I scanned the room for my friends. A lot of the mentors were already there, talking to one another, waiting for the career fair to start. They were all wearing special badges around their necks as a sign that they were allowed to be in the school.

Finally, I saw Faith sitting at the end of a table on her own. All she had was a carton of fries and an orange juice, which was her usual lunch. Actually, many of the girls at Buchanan ate the same thing for their meal. I don't know how they did it – if all I ate were fries, I think I'd go loopy with hunger. When she saw me, she smiled.

Cutting a path across the lunchroom, I couldn't help but notice that most of the students had stacks of Sebastian's colorful erasers, displayed proudly in front of them.

The corner of the cafeteria was packed with kids waiting in line at The Pit, excited that the collectable erasers were now being sold there. Every couple seconds, someone would walk away from the shop hollering about how they managed to get their hands on one. It reminded me of a midnight release at a video game store.

Jake and his wolf pack were sitting on the stage at the front

93

of the cafeteria, eating their sack lunches and pointing at random kids in the lunchroom, probably making jokes about their clothing or something.

I took the seat across from Faith, but before I could say anything, someone said my name behind me. "Chase?"

It wasn't a familiar voice so I wasn't nervous when I turned around.

A younger looking man, carrying a duffel bag, was walking through the cafeteria toward me. He wasn't one of the teachers at the school, and he wasn't someone I immediately recognized. "Yeah?" I asked.

"It's *me*," the man said, stopping in place and holding out his hands. "Miko!"

Without the makeup, he looked like a completely normal dude. "Hey, uh… Miko. Is Miko your real name?"

The clown without makeup set his duffel bag on the floor and took a seat next to me. "It sure is."

"So you're Chase's mentor for the week, huh?" Faith asked.

Miko nodded, setting a golden bicycle horn on the table.

I lowered my head, embarrassed.

"Before I get my gear on," Miko said, "I wanted to find you to let you know that a bunch of my friends will be here tomorrow. I told Principal Davis your idea about a bunch of us performing on Friday, and he *loved* the idea."

"*What?*" I said. "Dude, I was only *joking* about that!"

Miko was unfazed. "Oh? Huh. Well, they'll still be here tomorrow afternoon, so we'll be able to put on a killer show."

I shook my head, watching Faith's reaction from the corner of my eye. "Sounds *kind* of alright," I said, trying to be cool.

"I think it sounds *fun*," Faith said.

Miko sat up and smiled. "Thaaaank you," he said, and then he pointed his thumb at me. "Try telling *this* guy to lighten up a little."

"Dude, I'm *already* light," I said defensively. "I'm the lightest guy in the room, alright? I'm so light, I'm bright!"

Faith took a bite of her fries. "You're doing that thing again where you make no sense."

I lowered my head, but didn't say anything. I looked on the stage and saw Jake pointing and chuckling at me. Great. Now it was *me* they were making fun of.

Miko must've recognized how embarrassed I felt because he grabbed his duffel bag and stood from the table. He patted my shoulder once, and said, "See ya at the fair, kiddo."

Once he left, Faith laughed a little. "That guy seems pretty cool."

"Really?" I asked. "An adult that chose to be a clown seems cool to you?" I'm not sure why I was still being defensive about his career.

"Totes," she said with a mouthful of fries. "So what if he's a clown? He's probably just doing what he loves, a lot like a good friend of mine. He goes around the school wearing *ninja* clothes under his street clothes. He's even got a secret ninja clan that he trains with sometimes in some secret part of the school!"

I raised my hands, surrendering. "I get it," I said.

Faith took a swig from her orange juice. "We're all just doing what we love, aren't we?"

Just then, I felt someone bump into my back. I turned, expecting to see Miko again, but when I looked, there was nobody there.

"Sorry about that," said a boy farther down the aisle. The boy was wearing a hat so I couldn't see his face.

"No big deal," I said, waving my hand at him.

The boy didn't turn around, but waved back at me as he passed some students at the end of our table. They were busy stacking their colorful erasers in a line, and then knocking them over like dominos.

Turning back toward Faith, I caught a glimpse of Jake and the wolf pack again, sitting on the stage. They had finished their lunches and were throwing their own colored erasers at each other, like little kids trying to prove how hard they could throw something.

"Where are all yours?" I asked Faith.

She looked at the group of kids. "I could ask you the same question."

"I don't really know anything about them," I said. "I've been too busy with the whole bandit thing."

Faith groaned, understanding. "Well, I bought a couple of those things, but they weren't worth their weight in quarters. They're *terrible* erasers. They just smudged all my stuff instead of actually doing what they were supposed to do."

"Everybody seems to be in love with them," I said. "And you gotta admit, they *do* come in some pretty funky colors."

Faith paused. "If I cared about brightly colored rubber bricks, then I guess I'd have a whole stack of them to show off too, wouldn't I?"

That was the best part about Faith. It didn't matter what everyone else was doing – she made her own decisions about things, and the fact that she didn't have any block erasers meant she didn't care if people thought she was lame for not having any.

"I guess so," I said, casually looking around the students in the cafeteria. I swung my feet around to face away from the table, but something caught my foot. There was a small red book bag leaning against my leg.

"Is this your bag?" I asked Faith.

Faith leaned over and looked under the table. "Nuh-uh," she

96

said. "Is there a name on it?"

I hoisted the bag onto the lunch table, and inspected it. The zipper on the back unzipped a few inches from the weight of whatever was inside. "Not that I can see," I said, spinning the bag around. "It's heavy though."

"What's in it?" Faith asked.

"Books, probably," I joked, peeking into the opening on the side of the bag.

Suddenly I caught a whiff of spearmint. The stink was so strong that I flinched. And then I saw what was inside the bag.

It was filled with more packs of stolen gum.

I immediately pushed the bag shut and held it close to my chest.

"What is it?" Faith asked, concerned. "What's in the bag?"

"Nothing!" I replied right away. "It's *empty*."

"No it's not," Faith said, poking one corner of the book bag. "It's filled with *something*."

I was so freaked that I spoke without thinking. "Corn dogs! It's just a book bag filled with corn dogs! That's all! There's no incriminating evidence inside this bag that mysteriously showed up at my feet!"

I spun around in my seat and desperately searched the lunchroom for the kid who bumped my back only minutes ago. It *must* have been him! Why didn't I pay more attention when he ran into me? I even *talked* to him! I *talked* to the Buchanan bandit! He was in the palm of my hands and I let him get away!

"Chase, what's your problem?" Faith asked, leaning across the table and reaching for the bag. "Gimme that bag and show me what's going on!"

I jumped from the table and pulled the straps over my shoulders. "I know whose bag it is!" I said, lying. "So I'm just gonna head to the principal's office and drop it off! They'll probably make an announcement about it being in the front offices or something."

"Chase!" Faith said, frustrated and reaching across the table for me. "Sit back down!"

"Lates!" I said, saluting her. I turned and scrambled to the front of the cafeteria, keeping an eye out for the boy who ran into me. Was it Jake? No, because he was still on the stage when I got bumped. Unless he was some sort of alien that can teleport, it couldn't have been him, but that doesn't mean it wasn't a member of his wolf pack. I wouldn't recognize half those kids so if one were missing from the stage, then I wouldn't have known any differently.

I shuffled into the lobby of Buchanan, not sure of what my next move was going to be. Right at that moment, I saw Principal Davis walk out of the front offices with Coach Cooper at his side, and I panicked. I had enough evidence resting on my back to put me in detention for life, and I wasn't about to get caught with it.

Hanging a hard left, I headed for the boy's restroom just down the hallway. It was the restroom with a million different exits, one to the hallway, one to the boy's locker room, one to the gymnasium, and one to the cafeteria. If I got in a bind in there, at least I wouldn't be trapped in a corner.

I pushed the door open with my shoulder and stepped inside. The sound of rushing water came from a student washing his hands at the sink.

The boy looked at me in the mirror.

"Howdy!" I said.

My brain started screaming at me.

*What's the matter with you? Who says 'howdy' anymore?
In fact, who even makes conversation in a restroom at all?? Are
you trying to get yourself caught? Eyes on the floor and don't say
another word!*

The boy nodded, and pumped the soap dispenser.

When I'm nervous, it's impossible for me to keep my mouth
shut. "Washing your hands, huh?" I asked, pointing at the sink.
"Yeah, you'll really want to get that soap all bubbly. Did you know
it's actually the *bubbles* that clean the dirt off you? True story."

Stop it! He knows how to wash his hands!

And then I pointed to the air dryer on the wall. "You can
dry them off over there, good sir."

You're being too weird right now, even for you!

"Um, thanks?" the boy said, raising his voice like he was
asking a question. "But I prefer paper towels."

"Excellent choice," I said, watching as he pulled the brown
paper towels out of the metal contraption on the wall.

Finally, the boy stepped out of the restroom and I was alone.
I went into one of the stalls near the back and locked the door
behind me. Staring at the book bag, I got up enough courage to
look inside it again.

There had to be hundreds of packs of stolen gum, crammed
into the red canvas of the bag. Sitting at the top of the pile was a
folded sheet of paper.

I took it in my hands and unfolded it, expecting another
threat, but instead it said something else.

"Kind regards, the wolf pack."

It *was* the wolf pack.

A small chirp came from inside the bag, and then the
loudest siren I've ever heard started going off. The wolf pack had
set me up with a bag of stolen goods and an alarm to get
everyone's attention!

I freaked.

Stumbling back, I fell against the stall door and steadied
myself. The alarm was so loud that my head started hurting. I
thrust my hand into the bag and felt the small siren at the bottom,
but it had somehow been attached to the canvas itself.

I couldn't remove it so I did the next best thing. I stuffed the book bag into the toilet bowl, splashing toilet water all over the place, hoping the siren would short out from getting wet.

"OMG," I said, clenching my teeth. "I hope the last person who used this flushed!"

The blaring siren became muffled and started bubbling, but it was still going off. I gripped the bag tighter and thrashed it around at the bottom of the toilet until finally, it shut off.

I stood frozen, catching my breath, soaking wet, with my hands gripping a backpack that I had just stuffed into a toilet. Easily one of my top five *worst* moments at Buchanan, maybe even my *life*.

I set the wet bag on the floor, dragging it behind me as I stepped out of the stall. I didn't feel like things could get much worse.

But I was wrong.

I heard the front door to the restroom creak open, and

Principal Davis's voice echo across the tiles. "What in the *world* is going on in here? Who's back there?"

Not wanting to get caught, I ran to the side entrance behind the stalls, hoping that the door I chose would lead to the boy's locker room. Kicking the wooden door open, I jumped through carrying the wet book bag over my shoulders.

Stumbling over my feet, I fell to the floor, squeezing my eyes shut, afraid of getting hurt. The book bag slid to my side, dragging me along with it because of how heavy it was, making me roll to my back. I heard a few packets of gum bounce out of the bag, and then everything fell silent. I was glad too because I wasn't sure if I had chosen the correct door, but the fact that there wasn't any other sounds made me feel better... until I opened my eyes.

Lying on my back, all I saw were the upside-down faces of other sixth graders staring at me, the boy who just exploded out of the bathroom, dripping with water.

I had chosen the exit that brought me into the cafeteria, just to the right of the stage. I saw Jake and his wolf pack glaring at me, upside-down. When Jake saw the packs of gum on the floor, his eyes peeled open.

Hopping off the stage, he started to speak, but I immediately picked myself up and interrupted him.

"*Jake's* the one who's been stealing everyone's gum this whole week!" I shouted. "And he's been trying to set me up the entire time!"

Jake stopped in place with a shocked look in his eyes. His mouth was open, but he didn't say anything.

"See?" I said, pointing my finger at him. I let the book bag drop from my shoulders. It hit the cold floor with a gross splat. Unzipping the bag, I flipped it over, dumping out hundreds of wet packs of gum.

Everyone in the cafeteria gasped.

Wyatt suddenly appeared at the front of the onlookers, staring at all the gum on the floor. President Sebastian was right behind him, wearing a disgruntled looked upon his face.

Jake continued to say nothing, which surprised me, but the color of his face did a good job of letting everyone know he was getting angrier.

Again, I accused him. "He's been doing this all week! *He's* the gum bandit!"

Principal Davis stepped forward, looking at me up and down, probably wondering why I was soaked to the bone. He looked at Jake, and spoke. "Even though gum isn't allowed here, doesn't make it okay to take it." And then the principal addressed the crowd of students. "Has this been going on all week?"

Many of the students mumbled together.

"Why hasn't anyone said anything?" Principal Davis asked. He turned back to Jake. "Is this true? Are you stealing from your peers?"

Jake's face was as red as a beet. I almost expected steam to shoot from his ears.

"No!" Jake shouted. "It's not true! I mean, *yes*, I did it, but I was doing it because *wha*—"

"*Whyyyyy* can't you simply take the blame for what you've done!" Wyatt said, cutting Jake's sentence off. "You've stolen everyone's gum! It doesn't matter that gum isn't even allowed in the school! What matters is that *you* and *your wolf pack* are the

Buchanan bandits!"

Jake's clenched his fists, but he didn't argue. He shook his head, glaring at Wyatt, and then he looked at Sebastian for a moment as if waiting for the president to say something.

Sebastian lowered his gaze and turned away. Things were quiet and awkward for a moment.

It was weird.

Jake stepped forward and started to speak. *"Why aren't you—"*

Sebastian pointed his finger in the air. "To detention with you!"

Jake bit his lip, but said nothing else.

Principal Davis raised an eyebrow. "Thanks for *that*, but how about letting *me* handle this?"

Sebastian smiled. "Of course, I'm sorry. I was just getting carried away. You may take him away now."

The principal shook his head, sighing. "I've already had a long day, Sebastian, please don't make it any longer."

Sebastian nodded, still presenting his award-winning smile.

Principal Davis gestured for two of the hall monitors to clean up the wet mess from the book bag. Jake and his wolf pack all had to leave the cafeteria for questioning. Wyatt and Sebastian stood in the corner, shaking their heads or nodding every few minutes as they spoke to each other.

Before stepping out, the principal approached me. "I'll have a couple questions for you too in a little bit, Chase."

"How come?" I asked.

The principal shot me a look like I was crazy. "Because you're soaking wet with a bag *full* of stolen gum! Do you honestly think I'd miss a detail like that? You're obviously involved in all this somehow, and depending on what Jake says, I'll have more than a few words for you too."

I lowered my head. "Right."

Principal Davis sighed. "I know it's been a rough couple months here," he said softly. "But I'm just trying to make sure you're not mixing with the wrong crowd."

"Like chocolate milk and lemonade?"

"Like *what*?" The principal asked.

I shook my head. "Nothing."

I watched as Principal Davis walked out of the cafeteria. One of the hall monitors handed me a towel to dry myself off. Taking a seat on the stage, I ran the towel through my wet hair.

Faith, Brayden, Gavin, and Zoe sat beside me on the stage, watching as everyone began setting up for the career fair.

Faith was the first to speak. "So was that whole thing weird, or was it just me?"

Zoe nodded. "It was weird alright, but why? The bandit was busted, and the day was saved, wasn't it?"

Brayden shrugged. "Is it weird because we *want* it to be weird. Maybe in this case, it really *was* as simple as it turned out to be?"

"It feels like it was too easy," Gavin said, staring at nothing. "But most cases normally are. Most cases are just open and shut, much like this one. I say you take what you can get."

My friends all nodded their heads, agreeing with Gavin, but I wasn't so sure I felt the same. "Jake might've been the gum bandit all week, but *he* wasn't the one who planted the book bag by my feet."

Faith looked up. "But you never saw who *did* drop it, did you?"

"No," I said. "But I saw Jake on the stage about a second after that kid bumped my back."

"What kid?" Zoe asked.

Faith explained. "Someone bumped Chase's back, and apparently dropped the backpack full of stolen gum by his feet."

Zoe rolled her eyes. "Of course they did. I forgot this was *Chase* we were talking about."

I laughed. "But again, Jake was on the stage at the same time that kid dumped this bag by me, so it couldn't have been Jake! It's almost like someone's trying to frame Jake, which means somebody's trying to frame him *framing* me, if you can wrap your head around that."

"Why'd you accuse Jake to begin with then?" Brayden asked.

"There was a note in the bag," I said. "And it was signed '*the wolf pack*.'"

"There it is," Gavin said, nodding. "It wasn't *Jake* that put the bag there, but he got one of his minions to do it for him instead, so yep, Jake *was* behind it all the entire time. Sometimes you can get caught in a circle if you *over*analyze some things, y'know?"

Just then, President Sebastian raised his arms and started speaking loudly. "We've all had a pretty crazy week here at Buchanan School, but I think we can now rest easy knowing that the bandit has been caught!" He smiled at me, and pumped his first toward me like he was giving a speech. "And we have our very own Chase Cooper to thank for bringing the criminal to justice! Everyone give Chase a hand!"

The cafeteria full of students clapped their hands at the president's command.

Sebastian continued. "I wish I could hand out pieces of gum to celebrate Chase's heroism, but alas, the school *doesn't* allow gum!"

A few kids moaned, "Awwww."

Sebastian shut his eyes and held his hand in the air, waiting for everyone to quiet down. "But that doesn't mean we can't celebrate some *other* way. For the rest of the day, and *today only*, my block erasers will be *fifty* percent off!"

106

The entire cafeteria exploded in applause. It's possible that a couple kids died of heart attacks – probably not, but they sure were acting like they were going to. I think I even saw someone in the back gasping into a brown paper bag.

"Get your own block eraser right now in The Pit!" Sebastian shouted, but was barely able to get his voice above the shouts of hooray. "Check out the new color called 'wacky watermelon!' It *smells* just like watermelon!"

Zoe groaned. "Leave it to him to take this situation and make money off it."

"Oh well," I said. "As long as all the attention is off me, I'm happy with it."

I sat on the stage as my friends went back to their tables for the career fair. Nothing was adding up in my head no matter how I tried spinning the story, but maybe Gavin was right – it's possible that I was trying too hard to figure everything out when it was already figured out.

So *why* in the world was my gut telling me something was *still* jacked up?

Friday. 7:35 AM. Before school.

I got to school the next day hoping that everything would be back to normal. For all the other students of Buchanan, it probably was, but they also didn't know about the week I had just gone through. In fact, most of the kids here don't have a clue about *anything* that goes on behind their backs. It's probably better that way.

As I walked the halls to my locker, I couldn't help but notice the sound of incessant gum chomping. It was impossible to shut out the slurpy slurp sounds coming from nearly every kid I passed! Man, and I thought pirate jargon was annoying? This was turning out to be a hundred times worse! I guess with the bandit behind detention doors, everyone kind of went crazy with their gum.

What made it worse was that I was more tired than a sheep after getting sheared! Wait, sheep don't have to do anything when getting sheared, so maybe they're not tired after that. Whatever – you get it.

I didn't sleep the best overnight, mostly because I kept tossing and turning. I really wish I was the kind of kid who could push these thoughts out of my mind, but I just wasn't. It's my curse.

"Grand-master Chase!" Faith said, meeting me by my locker. "What's crackin'?"

I flipped the combination into the dial and swung the door open, leaning into the opening so all the garbage in the lower half didn't fall out. "I'm still bugged by all this."

Faith sighed, leaning against the locker next to mine. She watched the other students in the hallway. "Everyone seems to be cool this morning," she said. "The world is still spinning, nobody has to worry about getting stuff stolen, and everyone seems to be enjoying those little block erasers that Sebastian sells. The world has returned to normal."

Glancing at the other students, I saw that Faith was right. Nearly everyone in the hallway had more than a couple of the colored bricks in their hands. It even looked like a few people were trading with each other.

"Can't *wait* till *that* fad is dead," I said.

"Oh," Faith said sadly. She reached into the front pouch of her hoody and pulled out a bright blue eraser. "I actually got you one."

Faith got me a gift? If I told my parents that, they'd totally make fun of me for it, saying something like, "Looks like you two are gettin' pretty serious!"

"I'm sorry," I said smiling. "I didn't mean it like that. Those things *are* cool."

"Good," Faith replied, her face changing from sad to happy. She pinched the bright blue block and held it out at me. "I dunno. I just saw the blue one and thought you'd like it. Smell it! It even smells like blue raspberry!"

I held the eraser under my nose and took a big whiff. "Crazy," I said. "It really *does* smell like that. How is Sebastian able to make all these?"

"He probably buys them in bulk from somewhere," Faith said. "And then sells them at a higher price."

The first bell started going off. It was the warning bell, telling students they only had five minutes left to get to homeroom before school started.

Faith and I bumped fists, and each left for our separate homerooms.

Friday. 7:45 AM. Homeroom.

I managed to get into my seat just before the second bell stopped ringing. I don't know what it was about my classes, but I was always only able to make it by the seat of my pants.

Zoe spun around and spoke the second she knew I was there. "Something's not right."

I tightened a smile. "You feel it too?" I asked. "That whole thing with Jake is *still* bugging me."

My cousin looked at me, confused. Then she pointed at the blue eraser I had in my hand. "No," she said. "I meant that I could smell that eraser of yours. I thought you said you *hated* those things?"

"I did," I replied. "But they're starting to grow on me."

Zoe's eyes narrowed as she studied my face. She paused for a moment, but then spoke confidently. "*Faith* got it for you, didn't she?"

I laughed, nervous.

"Yeah," Zoe said grinning. "You're blushing. Faith gave that to you as a gift."

I think I got defensive because I was embarrassed. "No, she didn't."

Zoe paused again, watching my expression. "She did. She's so into you."

"Whatever!" I said. "No she's not. She was just being nice."

Zoe remained silent.

"Why?" I asked. "Did she say something?"

111

"No," Zoe said. "But she doesn't have to. I'm a girl, and can read these kinds of things."

Mrs. Robinson stood from her desk to make the morning announcements, but Friday announcements were always half-heartedly delivered. It was a pretty common attitude among all the staff, mostly because they were ready for the weekend.

Brayden leaned over in his chair. "You're still dwelling on that stuff from yesterday?"

I nodded. "Something about it just feels off, doesn't it?"

"Like there's more to the situation?" Zoe asked.

"Exactly," I said. "Like something's unfinished about it."

Brayden sighed. "I think I'm going to have to side with Gavin on this one, buddy. You might be digging too deep, trying to find a story where there *isn't* one."

I rolled the blue eraser on my desk, struggling to open my eyes because of how tired I was. "You guys don't feel it?"

Zoe shook her head. Brayden did too.

"Is your ninja-sense tingling?" Zoe joked. "Look, you saved the day for like, the *sixth* time! I say, put that notch in your ninja belt and be happy about it. Seriously. It's Friday, and the last day of the career fair, which means today is a total free day. None of our classes are gonna have any kind of work, and the last half of the day is just one big party. Isn't your mentor performing or something?"

"Yeah," I said, sinking in my seat. "He's got a bunch of his clown friends coming too."

Zoe curled her lip. "You might think it's lame, but I think it's super cool."

Brayden chuckled. "What if, instead of being a secret *ninja*, you were a secret *clown?* Training on your unicycle in some dark part of the school. No, wait, I just imagined that in my head, and I think that would probably scare the spew out of me."

Zoe and I laughed.

Mrs. Robinson finished with the rest of the announcements just as the bell sounded off again, and the students filed out of the room and onto the rest of their day.

Friday. 12:30 PM. Right before lunch.

The rest of the morning was easier to get through as soon as I decided to forget about the nagging feeling I had. The career fair was coming up, and I thought it'd be more enjoyable if my stomach wasn't rolling over itself from stress.

I saw Gavin outside the kitchen doors, standing in line for lunch, so I decided to join him.

"Hey," I said.

"Yo," Gavin replied, and then added. "Good to see that you're still in one piece."

I laughed, "Yeah," but then I stopped. "Wait, what? Why would I *not* be in one piece?"

"Because Jake is looking for you," Gavin answered.

"No, he's not," I laughed. "Good one, dude."

"No, really," Gavin said, looking somber. "I saw him walking around the halls this morning asking about you. He even asked *me* if I knew where you were."

"No, he didn't!" I said, desperately hoping that Gavin was playing a cruel joke on me. "There's no way he's at school today, not after yesterday! How is he not suspended, or at least in *detention?*"

Gavin shrugged. "Not every kid that gets in trouble is suspended. Some only get a slap on the wrist."

"Jake got a slap on the wrist for stealing everyone's gum?" I asked loudly, making every kid in line aware of our conversation.

My friend raised an eyebrow. "I got a few friends on the

inside still," he said, keeping his voice down. "And they said there wasn't too much evidence for Jake to get busted on. It was just that book bag filled with gum and a note signed from the wolf pack. Jake's parents threw a fit because there wasn't anything that proved he was 100% guilty."

I slapped my forehead. "Wasn't it enough that he confessed?"

"He didn't," Gavin continued. "My sources said he never actually said he was the one taking all the gum. Principal Davis had no other choice but to let him go, and I understand why."

"Because Jake might *not* have been the bandit," I said, finishing Gavin's thought.

"Booyah," Gavin said. "But I think it was pretty clear that Jake had *something* to do with it. Since Principal Davis doesn't know much about the situation, he still had to let Jake off the hook."

That feeling in my stomach returned, after I was *finally* able to let it go. The whole idea that something was still wrong weighed heavily on me all night because, in fact, there *was* something still wrong. Jake might not have been the bandit, but he was still a part of the bigger picture, but the problem was that nobody knew what the bigger picture was.

Friday. 12:40 PM. Lunch.

I sat in the corner of the cafeteria, watching the doors for Jake like a hawk. From my spot in the room, there was no way he could sneak up behind me. At least I hoped there wasn't – Jake *was* a member of the red ninja clan, and if anyone could sneak up on someone tucked into a corner, it would be them.

My neck started straining from the fact that I was sitting straight up and pushing myself into the corner.

A couple kids commented about how I was in "time-out," but I hardly cared since I was in the middle of being hunted.

Every couple of seconds, I found myself taking a deep breath. I guess my brain forgets to make me breath when I'm under stress.

I could tell my eyes were drying out because they would burn when I finally blinked. I was concentrating too hard on trying to see Jake before he saw me that I was beginning to feel exhausted, which was bad news on top of the fact that I was already super tired from my lack of sleep.

My head started bobbing as students became blurry. Squeezing my eyelids shut, I shook my head wildly, trying my hardest to stay awake. Every time I opened my eyes, my vision would sharpen, and I could see everything again, but only for about three seconds before my head bobbed again.

Faces became blurs of color, and voices became murmurs of nonsense, as a cold sweat chilled my body.

I set my head back against the wall and told myself it was

okay to rest my eyes, at least for a couple seconds. But when I opened them again, everyone was gone.

The cafeteria was completely empty. "Great," I said. "I slept through the rest of the day!"

The lunch tables had been folded and pushed against the far wall, and all the trashcans had been lined with clean garbage bags. The floor had been polished and gleamed like an ice skating rink.

I stood from the corner of the lunchroom, feeling a little upset that *nobody* had tried to wake me up, not even my friends! Zoe was gonna get an earful from me when I got home.

Walking to the double doors on the far end of the room, I heard the sound of something grinding along a hard floor. I spun around to see what was behind me, but there was nothing there.

The grinding came again, but this time from the hallway. Carefully, I stepped to the tinted glass windows and peered into the lobby of Buchanan, but there wasn't anyone out there either.

At least I didn't see anyone *human*. A line of aliens floated

down the hallway, winding down to a spot in front of the
Principal's office, where block erasers were being sold by a puppet
that kind of looked like Sebastian.

Strings were attached to Sebastian's hands and head, pulling
him back and forth, making it look like he was dancing. I looked
up, trying to see who was controlling the puppet, but the thread
disappeared in the shadows.

I watched a transaction take place, as one of the green aliens handed the puppet version of Sebastian some gold bars in return for a bright blue eraser. The alien giggled like a kindergartner, and then popped the eraser into its mouth.

"Sick," I whispered.

"Chase?" a voice asked, sounding like it came from an older man.

Chills ran down my spine. The voice came from behind me, from the cafeteria – the *empty* cafeteria! There wasn't anyone in there with me a few seconds ago! I had been alone!

"If it isn't Chase Cooper, as I live and breath!" the voice said again, apparently recognizing me.

I slowly turned, pushing my hands into my pockets to hide the fact that they were trembling.

The first thing I noticed was that the roof of the school had suddenly disappeared, and I was standing under a blanket of stars against pink and blue colors of the galaxy.

…what?

A man stepped forward, his face beaming with a smile. A black overcoat draped over his shoulders and covered a white dress shirt underneath, along with a big white bowtie. The coat stopped short in the front, but stretched out behind him, almost touching the back of his knees. The man looked like he was from an old fashioned movie.

"Lovely night, isn't it?" the man asked, looking at the stars. "The weather is *perfect*."

I wasn't sure how to respond, so I just grunted. "Mmm…"

The man paused when he saw my face. He stopped and held his hand toward me. "You *are* Chase Cooper, aren't you?" he voice boomed.

I nodded. "Who're you?"

The man put his hands out, and then pointed to his smiling face. He didn't say anything, trying to make me guess who he was.

I stared at him and finally shrugged my shoulders.

Again, he smiled, but this time bigger, and then pointed at his face another time.

"I don't know, dude," I said. "Do you work here?"

The man stood up straight and sighed. "It's *me!* James Buchanan!"

JAMES BUCHANAN

"Ohhhhhh," I said, leaning my head slowly back. I looked at the empty cafeteria under the twinkling stars. "So I'm dead then. I died. My afterlife is going to be spent in the empty hallways of Buchanan School while James Buchanan tries to make small talk with me."

James jumped back and put a hand on his chest. "Am I... *dead?*"

"Only by a few hundred years," I replied. "Hate to break it t'ya."

Buchanan walked over to the stage, and took a seat. He leaned forward resting his head in his hands. "Dead," he repeated softly in disbelief.

I walked up to the stage, feeling sorry for the old man.

Suddenly, he jumped forward with his hands up. "*Boo!*"

A very *not* manly sound came from my mouth as I hobbled backward and fell to the floor.

James jumped up and pointed his finger at me like an

120

immature child. "*Burn, sucka!* That's for making my mascot a *moose!*"

I had never felt more confused than I did at that moment. "*What?*"

James spun in a circle with his palms facing up, and then spoke like he was a surfer. "C'mon, *bro*," he said. "Look at the ceiling! It's gone, and you can see stars! You really think you *died?*"

I stopped. "This… am I *dreaming* this?"

Suddenly, fireworks erupted in the sky above the 15th president of the United States. "Boom!" he said, clapping his hands together. "You're dreaming, and I've been dead for *hundreds* of years!"

I remembered all the times I thought the ghost of James Buchanan had been messing with me. "Are you haunting the school?"

James raised an eyebrow. "Are you serious?"

"No," I said, immediately. "…sorta."

"No," James said, opening his eyes wide. "This is all in your crazy head right now."

"But why?" I asked.

"Because you probably fell asleep during lunch," James said, taking a seat on the stage again.

I hopped up, sitting by his side, and watching the line of aliens out the door. On the floor where I had been standing, giant puzzle pieces mysteriously appeared. They were scattered out of place.

"Got any gum?" James asked.

"No," I answered.

"No matter," James said, pulling out one of Sebastian's pink block erasers.

I shook my head, and joked. "Even if I did, the bandit probably would've gotten it by now."

"Ahhhh, yes, the *bandit*," James sang. "Whatever came of that?"

I decided to give in, and talk to James like he was a real person. Maybe it was part of my brain trying to talk to me, who knows? "The bandit was caught. At least, I *think* he was caught."

James raised his hand to stop me. "Start *before* that."

121

"Oh," I said. "Someone dropped a bag of stolen gum by my feet and—"

Shaking his head, James said, "Start before *that*."

"What, like the beginning of the week?"

James nodded.

I took a deep breath. "It all started on Monday. Some kids got their gum stolen, and I thought it was strange because it wasn't just *one* kid, but a whole bunch of them, and *only* their gum."

Two of the puzzle pieces on the floor connected on their own, making a clicking sound.

CLICK.

"Go on," James said, furrowing his brows as he listened intently.

"So I wanted to help find the bandit, but none of my friends did," I said.

"But you *did* get help," James added.

"I did," I sighed. "*Wyatt* offered his help."

A third puzzle piece slid across the tiles and attached itself to the other two.

CLICK.

"And to Wyatt, you said…" the president's voice trailed off.

"I said *no* at first."

"At first?"

"Yeah, because Wyatt and I aren't exactly besties, if you know what I mean."

"Surprisingly, I do," James joked. "So what made you team up with him in the first place?"

I thought about it for a second and remembered the boy's locker room. "Well, the bandit tried to frame me for stealing everyone's gum on Tuesday. He filled my gym locker to the brim with stolen gum."

Another puzzle piece attached itself to the group.

James nodded, staring at the stars. "And that's when you decided to team up with Wyatt?"

I shook my head. "No," I said, trying to remember. I stared into the pink and blue clusters of galaxies overhead. It was beautiful, almost as if I were floating through space. "There was a red ninja bracelet sitting on the bench behind me when I slammed my locker shut!"

Again, a puzzle piece moved into place. Five of them were connected so far.

"Right," James said. "And you know how secretive and protective Wyatt is when it comes to his red ninja clan, don't you? There's no way *anyone* in the red ninja clan would leave a bracelet like that lying around. That's such an uncovered track, especially for red ninjas who are experts at *covering* their tracks, right?"

CLICK.

Six puzzle pieces were connected.

"Wyatt *wanted* me to find it," I whispered, surprised that I hadn't seen the clue before. "It was so that I would remember the fact that he wanted to team up. He *needed* me to get scared of the stolen gum in my locker so that when I saw the bracelet, all I'd want would've been *his* help!"

James smiled, shooting a thumbs-up at me.

"But the *second* bag of gum…" I said, realizing the truth as I said it. "That happened *after* I told Wyatt that I was done searching for the bandit! He must've… he *did* it to scare me again,

123

didn't he?"

"Perhaps, but to scare you into doing what?" James asked. "The first time he used fear to team up with you. The second time, he used fear to…"

A few more pieces slid in place on the floor, but there were still nearly a dozen left sitting out in the open.

"To bust Jake," I said. "Wyatt kept on telling me that Jake was probably behind the theft, but *why* would he want to bust Jake?"

I watched the floor, hoping that another piece would move, but it didn't.

"That's the *bajillion* dollar question, isn't it?" James asked, chomping off one of the corners from the pink block eraser.

It was one of those moments when you know you're dreaming and something weird just happened, but at the same time you're like, of course that happened. It makes perfect sense that James Buchanan would take a bite out of one of Sebastian's erasers. And of course his breath would now smell like watermelon.

The remaining puzzle pieces trembled on the floor, like there was a brontosaurus stomping on the ground outside.

I stared at the half eaten eraser in the president's hand, and then remembered that the alien in the hallway *also* took a bite. My head started hurting as I tried to make sense of exactly what I was seeing.

James threw the rest of the eraser into his mouth, chewing it annoyingly.

"The *erasers*…" I whispered.

A puzzle piece slid into place.

CLICK.

The president blew a bubble until it popped.

I finished my sentence. "…are *gum*."

Fireworks erupted a second time in the galaxy above.

On the tiles below us, the puzzle pieces started moving on their own, taking their correct place on the floor.

CLICK. CLICK CLICK. CLICK.

My vision blurred as I stared at nothing, speaking quickly. "The erasers are Sebastian's product, right? The school is even selling them through The Pit! Kids are nuts over them, but not

124

because they're collectable erasers!"

CLICK.

"*But because they're gum!*" I exclaimed. "They're not *scented!* They're *flavored!*"

The puzzle was coming together on the floor in front of the president and me.

I continued. "Gum isn't allowed in school, but Sebastian found a way to sell it *without* the school knowing!"

CLICK.

"But what about Jake?" I asked.

The final puzzle piece connected, and I knew the answer. "Sebastian is in cahoots with the red ninjas," I said, still talking to myself as James listened. "It's *brilliant!* Sebastian gets the red ninjas to steal everyone's gum so that *nobody* has any! And then he sells it through the school so that *his* gum is the *only* choice they have! The staff was so fooled that even *they* were handing out free gum that they *thought* were erasers back on Tuesday! This is what Sebastian has been working on for the past couple of months!"

I stared at the puzzle on the floor. The image that it created was a kitten howling at the moon. "Um," I said, confused. "What's the deal with the howling kitten?"

James shrugged his shoulders. "I dunno," he mumbled. "It's *your* subconscious."

"But that just means you *should* know," I said. "Since you're *part* of my subconscious and all."

James grinned a sinister grin. "Are you sure that I am though?"

The stars began spinning overheard, shining brighter than they were before. Each drop of light grew larger until they were blobs, too bright to look at.

I covered my eyes with my hands, feeling them burn under my eyelids, but by the time I reached my face, the light was gone, and I found myself staring at Faith's face. Is that what they mean when they say someone was a sight for sore eyes?

"Was it werewolves?" Faith asked, flashing her cell phone in my eyes. "Were the werewolves chasing you again?"

I sat forward in my chair, realizing I was back in the cafeteria. My friends were huddled around me as I sat forward, still groggy from my power nap.

Reaching into my pocket, I pulled out the bright blue eraser that Faith had given me. Without thinking twice, I stuck it in my mouth and took a bite out of it.

My friends all freaked at the same time, shocked at my actions.

"*Sick!*" Faith said, gagging.

"What's *wrong* with you?" Zoe asked, covering her mouth.

Naomi raised her eyebrows and nodded, impressed.

Gavin finally chuckled. "Nice."

"Blue raspberry," I said, smiling with bright blue teeth. "This *isn't* an eraser. It's a chunk of blue raspberry bubble *gum*."

"Are you serious?" Zoe asked, lowering her voice. "These erasers are sticks of gum?"

Gavin's jaw nearly hit the floor. "Those things are everywhere!"

Naomi looked over her shoulder at the students in the cafeteria. "Which is exactly what Sebastian wants, isn't it? Those are his block erasers that he's selling through The Pit!"

I stood up, smiling at Naomi. She got it. She immediately understood what was going on. She was a good ninja, and I was glad to have her on my side. "The howling kitten puzzle comes together for you too."

"What?" Naomi asked, looking at me like I was crazy.

"Nothing!" I snipped loudly, embarrassed.

As my bad luck would have it, my loud voice got the whole cafeteria to look at me, which included President Sebastian.

"There he is!" I said, stepping forward, but stopped when I saw Jake and his wolf pack standing directly next to the president.

"Whoops," I said.

Sebastian snapped his fingers, and the wolf pack followed orders, dashing across the cafeteria in my direction.

All I could think about was that my friends were standing around me. I'd never forgive myself if any of them got hurt, so I started sprinting across the lunchroom, away from the people I cared about most.

Jake and the wolf pack were tearing their way toward me. The mixture of students and mentors were thick enough that they couldn't get to me as quickly as they wanted.

My nap must have lasted longer than I thought because most of the career mentors had already arrived and were setting up their display tables. I slid across the table where Gavin and Brayden's mentors were setting up.

As I landed on the other side, I snatched a bundle of rope

with a carabiner from the rock climber that had been paired with Gavin.

"Hey!" he shouted.

"I'll bring it right back!" I said. "Promise!"

Bursting from the cafeteria doors, I slowed down to look behind me. Jake was closing in, running at a full sprint. The principal's office was barely fifteen feet away. If I had time to think about it, I totally would've run in there, but instead I decided that using the zombies in the library was somehow the smarter decision. Don't judge me.

Swinging the rope over my shoulder, I jogged to the doors of the library, weaving my way around the students hanging around outside the doors. Glancing at one of the clocks in the lobby, I saw that lunch wasn't over yet, which meant that inside the library, smarties were still zombified.

Pushing the handle down, I slipped into the monster-infested room that I vowed never to return to.

Inside the cold library, it was silent, like *creepy horror movie* silent. As I tiptoed across the carpet, I heard the faint sound of buttons clicking away along with the low buzzing sound of vibrating phones, a sure sign that people in the room were texting.

Crouching, I hid behind a short bookshelf and snuck out to the center of the room. On top of the bookshelf at the very end was a cluster of colorful balloons floating silently. Someone must've gotten them for a birthday or something.

On the other side of the shelf sat the zombies I was so afraid of. I could hear their heavy breathing as they stared at their phones either updating a status or watching unbelievably cute kitten videos.

At the very center of the room were two staircases that joined halfway up to the second floor. It was much darker up there, and all I could see were the shadows of students, slouching at their tables, frantically typing messages to one another.

The door to the library burst open. Most of the zombies didn't notice, but I heard a few grunt out of curiosity.

Jake stepped farther into the library. Only two members of his pack trailed behind him, sniffing at the air, hunting for their dinner. Their actions were exaggerated because they knew people called them a wolf pack, and thought it was funny to actually *act*

128

like real wolves.

Scooting to the end of the bookshelf, I turned the corner. I had been in the presence of "library zombies" before, but it wasn't a sight I'd ever expected to get used to.

Kids sat at massive tables, staring into their phones, breathing out of their open mouths.

With faces glowing, they were hypnotized by whatever was on their five-inch touch screens, but still half-aware of the real world around them in case they needed to share their funny video with anyone who seemed remotely interested.

That was how their disease spread. That was how you got infected. *Zombies* infected by *viral* videos. *Viral.* Do you get it yet?

"Split up," I heard Jake whisper to his wolf pack.

His two wolves snorted their response.

I slowly pressed my back against the end of the short

bookshelf, keeping as quiet as possible. Any sudden movements, and I knew I'd be zombie fodder. I shook my head, feeling dumb because I thought the library was a good escape plan.

One of the zombies nearby peeked his eyes over the top of his cell phone.

I froze, watching the zombie's eyes scan over the top of the bookshelf. "*Please don't see me*," I mouthed. "*Please don't see me!*"

The boy's phone blinked at him, vibrating in his hand. "Rrrrrrrg?" he groaned. "Cute kiiiiitty."

I exhaled, thankful for still being alive. Leaning to my right, I glanced down the aisle to see how far Jake and his wolf pack were from me, but they weren't there. I turned my head to look down the other aisle.

"Rarhg!" a zombie growled, two inches away from my face. It was the same zombie that had been looking for me only seconds ago. He pointed his cell phone at me, and murmured. "Check out this video of a baby panda sneezing! You'll *die* from how cute it is!"

I tried rolling to my side, but the zombie grabbed my shirt and started whining. "C'mon, man," he hissed. "*Pandaaaaaas.*"

With all my strength, I freed myself from the zombie's grasp, but soon realized he wasn't alone. Hobbling to my feet, I saw that the other library zombies were stumbling out of their seats, pointing their phones at me.

"Not good," I said.

Jumping onto the short bookshelf, I sidestepped back down the aisle, careful not to lose my balance. And then I saw Jake and his wolf pack at the foot of the staircase. They turned when they heard all the noise too.

"There!" Jake shouted.

The two members of his wolf pack started sprinting through the room, dodging the zombified children of Buchanan School.

The crowd of kids was much thicker where I was standing. Zombie hands reached toward me like long branches on trees. I kept my vision at eye level so I wouldn't accidentally catch a glimpse of some funny viral video.

And then I stopped, feeling a light bulb switch on in my head. *Use your surroundings!*

I pulled myself on top of the short bookshelf and grabbed the small bundle of balloons. If TV and movies have taught me anything, it was that someone could hang onto the strings of helium filled balloons and float away to safety!

Snatching the strings that were attached to the brightly colored balloons, I held them at my side. "This has be a blast, but it's about time for me to catch some air!"

Everyone in the room paused for a moment, staring at the balloons in my hands.

Pressing my lips together, I shook the balloons in my grip. "Anytime now."

The zombies looked at one another, confused. A few of them had even started recording me with their cell phones.

I cleared my throat, pretty embarrassed. "So *that's* not something that actually happens," I said, releasing the balloons.

I CALL THIS ONE,
"MOVIES HAVE LIED TO ME."

As everyone watched the helium filled balls float to the ceiling, I jumped down from the bookshelf, and had another idea. I might not have been able to use the balloons as my surroundings, but I could use the *zombies* to my advantage.

Pointing my finger at the two members of the wolf pack, I shouted. "Those guys haven't seen that sneezing panda video yet! ZOMG, can you *believe* it?"

All the zombies turned at once. I heard several of them groan.

"Dude, you gotta see it! It's the funniest thing ever!"

"After you watch that, you gotta see this other video that's even funnier!"

"Yeah, man, those pandas are silly animals, but you ain't seen nothin' till you see the one with the kitty playing a keyboard!"

I expected the two members of the wolf pack to stop chasing after me, but they didn't even slow down.

With all the zombies dragging their feet toward them, I was clear to jump off the bookshelf. When I hit the floor, I took the rope off my shoulder, keeping one eye on the zombies and one eye on the wolf pack.

Weaving the rope around one of the solid table legs, I looped it back around and connected the carabiner to the other side. I ran through the crowd of kids until I made it to the front desk, where surprisingly, an adult woman was sitting and reading a newspaper like nothing was out of the ordinary. She even looked bored!

"You got a book you want to check out?" she asked with a nasally voice, chewing her gum loudly. Funny how teachers are allowed to chew gum.

"Uh," I said. "No, not today."

She waved her hand at me without looking up from her newspaper. "Then scram, kid. Can't you see I'm a little busy?"

"Sorry, ma'am," I said politely as I turned around.

The two members of the wolf pack were getting closer so I had to act fast. Pulling the rope tight, I looped it around one of the desk legs that the librarian was sitting at, and then I ran back *into* the crowd of zombies, yelling the entire time, "Check out this video I found of a *manatee* wearing a *ninja* mask! *What were you thinking, manatee?* That mask doesn't even *fit* you!"

My plan was that the zombies would chase after me, and then trip on the rope, creating a wall of fallen children that would separate the wolf pack from me. That way, I could simply walk out of the library, perfectly untouched.

The zombies began mumbling loudly as they turned toward me, desperate to see a manatee in a ninja outfit, which actually made me snort when I thought about it. Could you imagine that? A big ol' manatee decked out in ninja gear, sliding across the ice?

I shook the distraction out of my head, realizing the two boys in the wolf pack were too close for my comfort. I jumped forward and sprinted toward the front doors of the library again, doing my best to keep the zombies at a safe distance, but I had underestimated their desire to see a ninja manatee, and they were beginning to gain on me.

"Let me see that manatee!" growled a girl zombie as she shot her hand out toward me. *"Ninja manateeeeeeee!"*

I had to spin around to keep her from grabbing my shirt, but her fingertips still scratched my face. "Gah!" I said. "You guys are serious about your viral videos!"

Staggering backwards, I knew I was about to fall over, but thankfully I was back at the front of the library, where I had pulled the climbing rope across the ground.

From the corner of my eye, I caught a glimpse of the rope coming up. I tried stepping over it, but failed. It caught the back of my foot, and I was the first kid in the library that tripped on my own trap.

I hit the carpet hard, feeling it burn my elbows, and then I felt the weight of a hundred kids push into me as they tripped on the rope. The floor shook like an earthquake as more kids joined the pile.

I gritted my teeth, expecting to be covered by the zombie tidal wave, but actually found myself sliding farther *away* from where I had tripped. Since I was right at the front of the wave, I was getting pushed out.

Finally, I felt myself stop, coincidentally, at the entrance of the library. I stood, brushed myself off, and looked at the hoard of kids lying on the floor. The two members of the wolf pack who were chasing after me were laying in the middle of the mess, groaning in confusion.

"What. The. Heck," the librarian said sternly from her desk. I'm pretty sure I could see a vein throbbing in her neck. *"What the heck?"* she repeated, holding both hands over her hair like she was keeping herself from pulling it out.

It was when her eye twitched that I decided to slip out the door quietly.

Out in the hallway, the other students of Buchanan were going about their afternoon without a clue of the mini zombie apocalypse that had taken place in the library.

Across the lobby, I saw Principal Davis's office, but before I could start moving, the door to the library swung open, and Jake jumped out at me.

"You've been nothing but trouble for me!" Jake shouted, trying to tackle me.

I tripped across the short hallway just outside the lobby as kids stopped what they were doing to watch. I'm sure they were hoping for a fight, but I knew I wasn't going to be the one to give them a show.

Jake had both feet off the ground as he tried to get me to fall over, but I kept my balance the entire time. I'm sure that to everyone else, it just looked like I was carrying another dude on my back.

The cafeteria doors were right in front of me, which was the direction I was *trying* to fall in, but instead, I ended up losing my footing next to the doors that led to the costume department behind the stage.

With a painful thump, I fell into the entrance to the backstage, causing Jake to tumble over on top of me while I rolled across the dark room. I heard the wooden door click shut from behind me.

My stomach sank, knowing that Jake was alone in the room

with me. I was dead meat. I was so dead, they were gonna have to have a funeral for my *ghost*.

"Chase?" a voice asked from the corner of the dark room.

I picked my head up to see how Buchanan School was going to kick me while I was down. On the far side of the room, sitting at a dressing table, was Miko, my career mentor. He was in the middle of putting his makeup on.

I was about to say something, but stopped when I saw the shadows around my mentor begin to move. Some were short and fat, while others were long and spindly, stretching nearly fifteen feet off the ground. I wasn't sure what was behind Miko, but it was easily one of the scariest things I've seen in my life. And trust me, I've seen my share of scary things, most of which live in the dark pit of my locker.

"What's going on here?" Miko asked flatly.

Jake rolled to his back. His eyes opened wide as he scrambled to his feet. "Mind your business, clown!" he said, his voice shaking with fear. It was obvious that he was trying to sound like he wasn't scared. "This lame wad crossed the wrong kid, and he's gotta pay for it!"

Miko's eyes narrowed as he nodded, fully understanding the trouble I was in. He stood from the dressing table and folded his arms.

The shadows behind him moved again, and slowly walked forward and into the light. It was my mentor's friends, dressed in their clown gear. The tall spindly shadows turned out to be other clowns on stilts, hovering above everyone with their painted red smiles, but nobody was laughing.

Jake held out his shaking fist and squealed. "*I said stay out of it!*"

It's good to know that it's impossible for a bully to be a bully to everyone. It didn't matter how cool or how tough Jake was to the kids at Buchanan School, Miko wasn't going to have any of it.

"This kid bothering you?" Miko asked, staring into Jake's soul.

"He's trying to keep me from exposing the president of Buchanan for stealing a bunch of stuff from the students!" I said.

Looming over everyone, a clown on stilts honked his horn, but only once and slowly, making a "hurrrrrrrrrr" sound that eventually died out.

I felt like I was having a fever dream.

Jake spun in place and started moving toward the door, but a few of Miko's friends had already blocked off both exits in the room, one to the lobby and the other to the cafeteria. With stern looks upon their faces, they shook their heads at him.

Taking quick gasps of air, Jake stumbled backward. "No," he whispered. "I can't be here. I have an immense *fear* of clowns!"

"Then it looks like *someone's* in the wrong schoolyard," Miko said. I think he was curling his lip, but his huge red lipstick smile made it hard to be sure. Miko looked at me. "Get outta here, kiddo," he said. "We'll take care of your friend."

The clowns blocking the entrance to the cafeteria stepped aside and opened the door, allowing me passage through. I took one last look at Jake, who was glaring at me so hard that his eyes looked like they were glowing.

"This ain't over, Chase," he hissed. "Not by a long shot."

I smirked, stepping through the door and into the cafeteria.

The career fair had just started, and I could see Principal Davis standing with a huddle of other teachers all the way across the room. I was only about fifty feet away from finally being free from this disaster! All I had to do was reach the principal without getting into any more trouble.

That's when I saw Sebastian in the aisle next to me. We made eye contact, and then he snapped his attention at Principal Davis across the room, and then back at me. He did this a few more times – rapidly looking back and forth between the principal and me.

The president took off running as fast as he could down the aisle. I flinched, confused about what to do, but then bolted like I was competing in a shuttle run.

Sebastian was taller than me, with long legs that made his sprint look easy, and widening the gap between us. It was everything I could do to even keep up with the kid.

Students dove out of the way when they realized I was shredding down the aisle at full speed, but I still shouted to warn them. *"Gangway! Move, move, move!"*

I kept my eyes forward, but could see that I was passing Sebastian, and could hear his heavy panting fall behind me.

Principal Davis was getting closer and closer as I struggled through the cramp in my side.

This was it. I was going to tell Principal Davis the whole story, and nobody was going to stop me.

Slowing myself in front of the Principal, I tried talking, but my throat was so dry that I could only choke out a cough.

The principal turned his attention toward me. "You okay?" he asked.

Suddenly I felt a hand grip my arm and tug me to the side. I tripped over my feet, stumbling away from the principal. With my eyes, I followed the arm that was pulling me aside, and saw that it belonged to Wyatt.

"What are you—" I started.

Wyatt interrupted me. He pointed at the principal. "Just watch."

Principal Davis was still looking at me when Sebastian slammed into him at full speed the same way a linebacker tackles a quarterback. Both of them fell through the huddle of teachers until they smashed against the brick wall with a sickening thud.

The principal shook his head, and looked at Sebastian. "Are you okay?" he asked, genuinely concerned. "What happened? What's going on?"

Sebastian stood up immediately, speaking at light speed. "Don't believe whatever it was that Chase just said to you! The gum I sell in The Pit is *good* for the school!"

The principal stared at Sebastian, clearly shocked.

Sebastian was still panicking, and must have misread Principal Davis's silence as an invitation to keep running his own mouth. "It's *good* for business," he continued. "Even *you* said the added money in the budget was a *good* thing! Sure, I might've gotten a couple of kids to do the dirty work of stealing gum in the school, but that was all necessary for my plan to succeed! And yes, my erasers are blocks of bubble gum, which really isn't such a bad thing when you remember how much *money* I've made – I mean, money that the *school* made."

The students fell silent as Sebastian spoke like his volume was stuck all the way up.

"Gum *isn't* allowed at this school, alright?" Sebastian said, starting to sound like a lunatic. "And I will *not* stand by and watch as students sneak packs of gum into class! If you *want* to chew on bubblegum, then you *have* to buy a pack from me, which is *only* available from The Pit!" Sebastian stopped talking to catch his breath. He turned to Principal Davis. "So you see? Whatever Chase said doesn't even matter! We're investing in *our* school's future with my gum."

"Chase didn't say *anything* to me," Principal Davis said flatly.

"Um," Sebastian said, staring into space with wide eyes. Something must've snapped in his head when he realized he confessed to the entire scheme. "Uh-oh."

With a cold stare, Principal Davis put his hand on Sebastian's shoulder, escorting him to the end of the cafeteria. It

140

was over. All of it had ended when the president of Buchanan said too much. His whole plan that he had been working up for the past few months had just crumbled at the weight of his own words.

SEBASTIAN'S "UH-OH" FACE.

I took a breath, savoring the victory, and then started to walk toward the principal, but felt Wyatt grip my arm again. "Let go, will ya?" I said, super annoyed.

"*What* do you think you're *doing?*" Wyatt asked.

"I'm gonna tell Principal Davis about everything I know," I replied, yanking my arm away from Wyatt. "Sebastian just confessed so it's probably best if I'm there with my side of the story too."

Wyatt paused, his evil grin stretching across his pale face once again. "You think Principal Davis is going to listen to you? After all, you were *part* of Sebastian's scheme."

I felt my face grow hot. "What are you talking about?"

Wyatt snickered. "Don't forget the box of Sebastian's 'erasers' you delivered to the front offices on Tuesday."

My stomach dropped. Wyatt had given me that box to deliver to the staff as a sign of faith. "You set me up!"

"Of course I did!" the leader of the red ninjas said. "I need some extra dirt on you to make sure you keep your place at the bottom of the food chain. So if you say *anything* to the principal, I'll remind him of your '*special*' delivery."

My fists were so tight that my palms started to burn. "This was all part of your plan," I said.

Olive stepped beside me and took Wyatt's hand. She stuck a piece of gum in her mouth, and then snickered. "Hey, babe."

Wyatt grinned.

Olive glared at me. "Wyatt's gonna be the new *president* of Buchanan," she said.

The room started spinning as I realized Olive was right. Since Wyatt was the vice president of Buchanan, that meant he was next in line for president if something ever happened to Sebastian. And by the way Principal Davis looked as he spoke to Sebastian, there was *no way* that kid was still going to be president.

Wyatt stepped onto one of the lunch tables and cleared his throat. "Ladies and gentlemen," he said. "As your new *president* of Buchanan School, I'd like to be the *first* to tell you that—"

"Not so fast!" Principal Davis said from the side of the cafeteria. Sebastian was in the hallway, waiting with a hall monitor as the principal stepped closer. "This isn't like the actual presidency."

Wyatt jumped off the table.

"There's clearly something fishy going on," the principal continued, and then he gestured to the career mentors scattered around the room. "But since there are professionals in the building today, it'll all have to get sorted out first thing on Monday morning."

Wyatt walked past me, bumping my shoulder. Olive was attached to his other hand as they marched back to their table for the career fair. I'm sure he was fuming at the fact that Principal Davis just set him in his place. Good thing too, or else everyone would have to take orders from *President Wyatt*. Gross.

For a second time, I allowed myself to breath deeply. Even though things were still shaky, everything was at least under control again. I sat at one of the tables as my friends joined me.

"Um," Faith said with a cocked eyebrow. "So that was the craziest thing I've ever seen."

Brayden leaned forward. "At least *Wyatt's* not president," he said. "Can you imagine? Wow. Just... *wow.*"

"There was a second where I thought he *was* going to be president," I said. "What do you think's gonna happen to Sebastian?"

Gavin answered. "Stripped of the presidency for sure, but nothing much after that. Slap on the wrist, maybe." He looked at Zoe. "This might call for another election, y'know. My bet is that Principal Davis will just reset the entire system, like a game."

Zoe laughed. "Fun! Election *weeeeeeeeek!*" she sang.

"So is Wyatt really that much of an evil genius?" Naomi asked, bringing the room down again.

Everyone looked at her, unsure of what she meant.

"What do you mean?" I asked.

"I mean, Wyatt had a master plan this entire time," Naomi said. "A master plan that was *behind* Sebastian's master plan. Like, we know Wyatt and the red ninjas were working with Sebastian for the past month."

"Longer than that," Brayden said, correcting her.

"But the entire time that Wyatt was taking orders from Sebastian," Naomi continued, "he was actually figuring out his own plan to become the president. He figured out how to weasel his way to the top! And he played you – *both* of us, this entire week!"

Everyone nodded, listening to the girl from my ninja clan.

"He had his sights set on Jake the whole time," Naomi said, chuckling in disbelief. "Wyatt *needed* Jake to take the fall so he wouldn't have to. If the vice president of the school were to get caught stealing gum, he would get fired from being VP."

"That's why he was so pushy about making sure we knew Jake was responsible for the stolen gum," I said.

Faith sat at one of the tables, sinking down. "He really *is* a genius."

Zoe folded her arms. "The good news is that he's *not* the president," she said. "So we can all sleep soundly tonight."

"Jake was just a pawn this whole time," I said, and then suddenly remembered he was with Miko. "Wait a second... *what happened to Jake?*"

At that moment, all the kids in the cafeteria burst out with

143

laughter. They were pointing at something near the front of the cafeteria, but I couldn't see what it was through the crowd of students.

The sound of a clown's honking horn bounced off the walls as my friends and I made our way to the front.

There, sitting on the edge of the stage, was Jake, leader of the wolf pack, member of the red ninja clan, quarterback of the Buchanan Moose football team… and he was painted up like a circus clown.

CLOWN JAKE

"We didn't make him do it," Miko said, suddenly standing behind me as if he materialized out of nowhere. "He *offered* to do it."

"He actually *wanted* you to paint his face?" I asked.

"Yep," Miko said. "He said he would walk out of the room in a clown outfit if we left him alone."

"What were you *going* to do to him?" Naomi asked.

Miko laughed. "Absolutely nothing! We were just going to let Chase get a couple second head start so he could make it to the principal without getting hassled!" Miko spun around and scanned the room. "Looks like you took care of business too, kiddo."

"Thanks," I said. "Hey look… I'm sorry for being hard on

you this week."

Miko raised his hand. "No big deal. I get it from everyone."

"The point is that you're a super cool dude," I said. "You do what you do because you love doing it, even when dorks like me give you a hard time for doing it."

"It's all about shutting the dorks out, right?" Miko joked. "I'm sure you have to do that all the time when you're parading around as a ninja."

My mouth dropped open, shocked. My friends slightly gasped around me too.

"How did you know?" I asked.

Miko didn't answer. He just smiled like he was hiding a secret, and then winked at me before walking away.

"That dude is good," Naomi said.

My friends hung around for a couple seconds after Miko left. We joked about the tough week it had been, and made fun of each other for a bit. I was the one they were picking on the most, but I didn't mind. They were my friends, and it was cool. The way they were goofing on me made things feel normal again, like we were just a group of kids with normal sixth grader problems.

The cafeteria began buzzing with activity as everyone in the school went about their normal routine for the career fair. Funny how quickly things can settle down, even after a weird confession is screamed across the entire room by the school's president.

Another week at Buchanan and another bully busted. A ninja might not take breaks, but this ninja does. It's not easy getting through a week like that without anyone getting hurt, but I managed to do it. And that's a pretty impressive ninja skill, if I do say so myself.

Zoe, Brayden, Gavin, and Faith returned to their seats. Naomi stood by my side. This week was the most time I've spent with her, and even though she was a good ninja, I learned that she was an even better friend. She never left my side, not even when things got tough. No, *especially* when things got tough.

"Thanks," I said.

Naomi looked at me, confused. "For what? That was a little vague."

"For sticking by me," I said. "It really means a lot to me."

Naomi slugged me on the shoulder, in the exact same

145

stinkin' spot that Zoe had a couple days ago. I did my best to keep from flinching, but the only way I could do that was to force a smile and squeeze my eyes shut.

Naomi laughed. "Sorry about that," she said. "I'm just… I'm bad at responding to compliments. What I *meant* was… you're welcome, but don't mention it. You don't need to thank me for being your friend."

Just then, I felt a tug on my elbow. I turned, expecting to see Wyatt again. I was happy when I saw that it wasn't him. It was a shorter boy who I only recognized from the hallways between classes. "Hi?" I said, accidentally making it sound like a question.

The boy didn't say a word. He simply handed me a folded note, and briskly walked away as if he were afraid.

"That can't be good," Naomi sighed. "What is it with kids at this school and notes? Why doesn't anyone communicate with their mouths, *like normal human beings*?"

"Right?" I asked, opening the sheet of paper. The writing on the note was typed, which somehow made it feel creepier. I read the words aloud, but quietly.

"You've crossed the line this time and have awoken a sleeping giant. You have been warned. The storm is not coming…

it is already here."

"Wonderful," I whispered. "I guess the Scavengers *are* real."

Naomi spun so fast that she almost tipped over. Frantically, she scoured the room. "The Scavengers? Did you seriously just get a note from The *Scavengers?*"

I scanned the cafeteria for the boy who delivered the note, but he was nowhere to be seen. Crumpling the sheet of paper in my hand, I glanced at my friends who were only a few tables away. "It sounds like more of a warning."

Zoe looked up from the group and waved at me to come over. I took a deep breath, and exhaled slowly.

The Scavengers might've been the real deal, but there was no way they were going to take this victory away from me. I tossed the note into one of the garbage cans along the wall as I started walking toward my cousin.

"You're just going to throw that away?" Naomi asked, jogging to catch up, still keeping an eye out over her shoulder.

"Why not?" I replied.

"I… because…" Naomi paused. "Huh. You're right. Why not?"

"Their message was delivered," I said. "But I don't care."

"You don't?"

I shook my head. "Not today at least. We just won a huge victory over Sebastian and Wyatt, and I'd like to savor that for the rest of the day. I think I deserve that. I mean, I think *we* deserve that, don't you?"

A smile appeared on Naomi's face. "You know, I think you're right." She wagged her finger at me and spoke again. "I *knew* there was a good reason you were the leader of the ninja clan. Too bad it's taken me this long to figure it out though. Maybe next time you can be insightful a little *quaster*."

I faked a laugh, remembering when I smooshed the words 'quick' and 'fast' together. "Mwah hahaaaa, very funny."

Once we got to our table, I took a seat between Faith and Zoe. Naomi sat on the end of the bench next to Brayden. Everyone was smiling except for Naomi and me.

Part of me wanted to tell my friends about the note from the Scavengers, but a bigger part of me was glad they didn't know. They could at least enjoy the rest of the day without the stress of new threat looming over their heads. That bad news could wait until later.

I took one more look behind me, just to make sure there wasn't anyone there. Y'know, like maybe another kid with a note, or a member of the red ninja clan, or one of the Scavengers, or the fifteen president of the United States, or even the white ninja.

Man, Buchanan School was a *stressful* place, but I shook the strange feeling from my shoulders and forced myself to smile – you'd be surprised at how *making* yourself smile has the power to brighten your day, even if it's just a little bit. And I had plenty of reasons to smile. No matter how crazy my life was, there wasn't anywhere else I'd rather be than in the cafeteria with my best friends.

Faith tapped my hand with her finger. "Everything okay?" she asked softly.

"For now it is," I said with a smile. "For now it is."

Stories – what an incredible way to open one's mind to a fantastic world of adventure. It's my hope that this story has inspired you in some way, lighting a fire that maybe you didn't know you had. Keep that flame burning no matter what. It represents your sense of adventure and creativity, and that's something nobody can take from you. Thanks for reading! If you enjoyed this book, I ask that you help spread the word by sharing it or leaving an honest review!

- Marcus
m@MarcusEmerson.com

THESE BOOKS ARE MORE AWESOME THAN TWO SCOOPS OF VANILLA ICE CREAM IN A FROSTY MUG OF ORANGE SODA! HAVE YOU EVER HAD THAT? IF NOT, THEN YOU SHOULD TRY IT BECAUSE IT TASTES **SUPER AWESOME!**

Marcus Emerson is the author of several highly imaginative children's books including the 6th Grade Ninja series, Secret Agent 6th Grader, Lunchroom Wars, and the Adventure Club Series. His goal is to create children's books that are engaging, funny, and inspirational for kids of all ages - even the adults who secretly never grew up.

Born and raised in Colorado Springs, Marcus Emerson is currently having the time of his life with his beautiful wife Anna and their three amazing children. He still dreams of becoming an astronaut someday and walking on Mars.

Made in the USA
San Bernardino, CA
20 February 2018